A Mistake

The air had chilled as late fall struggled to survive the incoming of winter. Children giggling and tired from wandering the streets as goblins and ghosts were safe in their homes with their bags full of scrumptious goodies. Past the hour of darkness, only lit pumpkins gave a glow to the witches' night of capture named Halloween.

Kat (short for Katherine May Forrester), at 5'5" tall, scrunched her womanly curves into a fetal position in the trunk of an old Buick that was now heading out of the small rural town of Lexville. Her brown eyes wide with fear and thick, muddied and ratted brown hair matched the dirt streaks across her paled face. Frightened and shaking violently, she could barely make out muffled sounds coming through the back seat. The air was getting thinner and much hotter as she gasped under the tape covering her mouth. Sweat beads were streaming into her eyes, burning and making it more difficult to keep them open.

A distant whistle of a train told of one more clue as to which direction she was being taken. Kat concentrated hard to hear over the loud hum of the car and road noise. The dissipating oxygen level and the stench of mildew, old socks, and stale body odor were overwhelming. Paying attention was getting harder by the minute. Not to mention the pure adrenaline of the situation. After the mind-racing shock of being grabbed and thrown into a car trunk. Kicking and fighting rendered useless, she needed to pay attention to every sound passing.

To herself, she reasoned, *YES! The annual All Hallows derby car auction! I can just barely hear a loud speaker. We have to be passing the old auction grounds. The train went by after the loud speaker. That means we're headed west and out of town.* Stomach tied in knots, she mused, *Not good, this means the clues will run out. TIME, yes, hard to guess how long without my cell phone. I must have dropped it in the scuffle. The radio, I can almost make out with a break in the background noise. Songs are approximately three to four minutes each and announcer time maybe a couple minutes.*

"Hey, Jo, what do you think? Prime, eh?"

Jo Bud Baur, a tall and powerful man, with dark, slicked hair, glanced over at his brother with disgust. "That was stupid." Looking back at the road with serious eyes. "One of these days, you will need to be dealt with."

From the shorter, pudgier brother that resembled their Ma: "Oh come on, Jo, it's Halloween. At least she finally stopped kicking, maybe she passed out."

Jo again: "This one can never go inside." A pause of threat. "You hear me?"

Pudge, as everyone called Billy Jud Baur, smiled a brush-off. Jo drove the rest of the way home in silence.

"Okay, everyone"—which consisted of a house of seven at present, including Jo and Billy's Ma or Alicine Fair Baur. Everyone that became part of the family referred to Ma as Miss Mam. A burly woman, with long tresses of graying, once-blonde hair commanded in a motherly tone, "Let's get the supper table set so we can be ready for Jo and Billy to get back from town."

Samuel Shin Lafray, a very well-mannered gentleman in his thirties, with shaved hair as dark as his midnight skin, nodded with an enthusiastic "Yes, ma'am!" Beside him stood Harrold Lou Graden, an aged, quiet sort of a man with a long ponytail of grayed hair, and eyes that resembled the afternoon sky. Harry bowed his head quietly as he laid out Miss Mam's lacy tablecloth. Cara Lai Ofranks, a rather thin, tall, red top, and Darci Rose Redimere, a plump brunette, grabbed the dishes. They all pitched in and did their part to help out. As the Good Book says, according to Miss Mam, Taketh, giveth, and we shall receiveth. She preached that to everyone that came through her door, and even those who came to her door. Miss Mam, had a sweet kind of voice, which did well at disguising her demand for control and respect.

She is a woman you just don't say no to. She kept everyone in the house fed and minding their manners. "Is that Jo and Billy I hear?"

"Yes, Miss Mam," said Sam.

"Well, all right, then, let's get the food on the table while they tend their business."

Jo and Billy entered through the back door and put up their coats as Ma gave them that "better be doing your job" stare. Jo gave her a serious nod and they all sat down to supper, praying with hands folded as Ma read the same piece out of that book she calls her bible every evening.

Fright turning to anger, tears pushed at Kat's eyelids as she fought the urge to succumb to the overwhelming feeling of hate and disgust. Still mumbling under tape so tight on her mouth it hurt, she thought, *if they put their grimy hands on me one more time!* Looking around the room they'd laid her in, there was only one way out. It was locked on the outside and Kat could hear the humming of equipment. *What is this place?* The floor was dirt, and the room was completely empty. *They put me in a shed?* Scared, mad, and hands still bound with rope, Kat scooted to the far corner of the room and curled into a ball and wept.

The town of Lexville was nestled in a quaint valley at the foot of stout hills. Being what most locals called a seedling of

Canada, even though it was nowhere near the border of Canada. The streets now quiet of trick or treaters, parties of much older goblins were now streaming through residents' windows and doors as witches' guffaws and music carried on. Kyra Tay Banks, a tall thin gal with such straight champagne hair, it deemed her a pole, stood looking around the room for the familiar face of her best friend. Everyone seemed to be having a good time and drinking way too much rum punch. Locating a large group of Kat's coworkers, which were also her friends as in a small town, everyone knows each other well.

Kyra dipped into the circle with a polite smile and questioned, "Is Kat working late?"

A woman who works in the same office with Kat spoke up, "No, isn't she here?"

Kyra said, "I haven't located her yet. I was going to pick her up, but she said she wanted to walk over so she could hand candy out on the way."

The woman gave a nod of agreement. "Oh yes, she did mention that. I'm sure she's here somewhere by now. Check the lady's room around the corner. There's been a line there all night." Kyra gave a smile of thanks and scoped the line and the rest of the house. Having no luck, she tried her cell. Getting no answer, Ky slipped out the front and headed on foot toward Katherine's apartment building. The streets still lit with pumpkins the whole way, gave a bit of a sinister feeling in the gut as Ky got closer to the complex and saw no Kat anywhere.

Climbing the back stairs to the second level of the triplex apartment, Kyra used her key to enter and called out, "Kat? Are you still here?" Walking through the entirety of the apartment, which consisted of three levels, Ky thought to herself, *She has way more space than she needs in here.* Ky called Kat's cell again. This time letting it go to her voicemail. "Hey, girl! just wondering if you dumped me for some sexy man tonight! call me soon, Ky, kisses!" then hung up and headed back to the party.

Kat's eyes opened in a panic, as she realized she had dozed off from traumatic exhaustion. Air was streaming in but no light between old rotting wood planks that felt like the dead of darkness. Hair already ragged and face dirty from her hobo costume, she closed her eyes, and took a deep breath in to find a moment of calm. The realization of the predicament was overwhelming. She had been locked in this shack for hours. Hard to believe she could sleep at all. At least they had thrown an old dirty wool blanket over her. It's not exactly that warm in late October! *Asking God, "WHY?" is not going to help.* Praying for strength and one thousand angels was her only choice.

Trying not to think of what these guys will do to her, Kat looked around again, but slower and more determined. Thinking, *Lord please help me find a way out. No one knows where I am.* By the door, Kat spotted a piece of broken wood sticking out. She leaned on the wall as she slid up to standing as a splinter forced itself into her right shoulder blade.

"Dammit!" she mumbled under the tape. *So maddening! I can't even swear out loud!* On weak legs, Kat made it over to the door, turned around, and tried to get her hands high enough so the rope would catch on the fat splinter of wood. "SHIT!" The door flung open and the taller, meaner of her two captors, came in. Kat swore again under her breath as the door hit her in the head. Then slid to the floor and stared at the man with vengeance crossing the whole foot of distance between them.

"I brought bread." Then he grabbed her arm lifting and turning her around in one smooth jolt. He unwound the rope and held both her arms behind her. He pulled out a knife and stared into her eyes with assurance. "Try to run and I'll use it," he warned as he ripped the tape off her face. "Not a word." Kat said nothing and took the bread as she would need strength for the task coming. "Eat it now." Jo stood waiting. Kat chewed the bread as fast as she could. He then pulled a small bottle of water out of his coat pocket and handed it to her. "Drink." She did as she was told and then stared into his eyes. It was like staring into the wild eyes of a rabid wolf.

So cold it brought bile up from somewhere deep in her gut, and before she knew it, she was bent over heaving. "Son of a bitch!" The man yanked her to the other side of the shed and pushed her down. Kat huddled in the corner and waited to see what he would do next. He retied her wrists with the rope and stuck the same dirty piece of tape to her vomit dampened mouth. He cussed some more then reached out the door, grabbing an old metal pail. He threw it in the corner and pointed. "Your toilet for now." He left, relocking the door, then quiet. With a frightened sigh of relief, Kat gave a shudder and thought to herself, *at least he didn't rape and torture me ... yet.* She waited a good ten minutes before trying again, rubbing the rope as best she could against the wood splinter.

Jo headed to the barn where he caught up with Pudge. "We've got to double secure these out buildings again now that we have a newcomer." Pudge agreed with a nod and got busy with boards and padlocks.

"Ain't nobody supposed to be coming in our barn, Jo."

Jo turned and lit a cigarette staring at the shed just yards from the barn. "Yeah, well, this one's a little different. Just make sure it's secured well." With that he headed back to the house.

FREE! Kat breathed an adrenaline rush as she wriggled her hands free of the rope. Pulling the tape from her mouth and with determination settling deep, she dropped to the floor. Digging desperately at the dirt, under the door, she held her hand at the bottom of the door and whispered to herself, "There is air coming in!" Still whispering low, "Please, Jesus, help me get out!" Digging with cold hands the air started coming in heavier. Grabbing the bottom of the door and shaking, it rattled. Kat stood up and rammed her body weight against the old door. Stopping to listen, then jarring the hinges loose one more ram at a running start should do it. And so she did. The door now hanging solely by one side and the hinges broken, Kat landed on the ground half in and half out of the opening.

Looking around and lying very still, Kat could see the big farmhouse to the west and a very large barn just yards behind her. The house was quiet. Scrambling to her feet, she took long strides but very slowly and keeping low. Kat reached the edge of the woods. Crouching down behind some holly bushes that lined the side of the yard, she started scanning the place. She was only there a moment when a man's loud whisper startled her.

"Hey!" She cringed, then whirled around to see a man about thirty something, clean shaven, stocky, black as night. "Whattaya doin out here, ma'am?"

Staring, and waiting for her heart to get back into her chest, Kat answered in a very quiet whisper, "I was abducted by two guys and put in a shed."

A curious look on his face, "Well, I don't rightly know about all that." The man put out his hand in a gesture, "My name's Sam. I live here." He shifted to his other leg and looked at the ground hesitating. "I don't want to misspeak, but I'm not too sure anyone around here would put someone in a shed." Scratching his head. Those two sons a hers keep a close eye on things."

Kat angered instantly. "Yes, well, two guys nabbed me right off the street."

Then in a sudden shout from the house: "Son of a Bitch!" Kat and Sam both jumped and turned. It was Jo, the taller, meaner-looking brother. Sam seemed to have frozen. Not sure why Jo was all caught up in anger. Kat, stared with vengeance. The look he returned was of a silent threat. Jo did look angry, but he turned to Sam and softened a little, not wanting to cause a commotion, but then a holler came from behind the three.

"What's going on out here, Jo?" demanded a burly, grayed woman coming from the house.

Jo rolled his eyes and turned to look at his mother. "Nothing, Ma, just found this girl out here wandering on the property."

Kat, exasperated, yelled "WANDERING?" before Jo could get another word in. The well-aged woman looked very suspicious, but she put on a smile and gave Jo a look of seriousness with her eyes that bade, *I'll deal with you later.*

She, Ma, turned to Sam and said, "Well, come on now, Sam. We need to get you back to your room. Jo can handle all of this."

Sam gave the whole situation a puzzled look. "My, my don't know about all this."

Miss Mam turned back to the girl in her yard. "And Miss Lady," she said, putting her arm out towards Kat, "you look like you could use a dish of stew and a bath."

Kat looked and pointed at the man, Jo. "He kidnapped me!" Still looking toward Jo, she added, "Take me back to town. Now!"

Miss Mam put her arm around Kat's shoulder and guided her toward the house as if soothing a wounded child. "We will just get you set up with a room and, oh my, we need to get you into a hot bath. You poor dear, probably don't have a decent piece of clothing. Then you can tell me all about it."

Kat, rolling her eyes, said, "Actually, ma'am, I need to get to town. I have to get home." Trying to talk faster, she added, "People will be looking for me! Where is your phone?"

This woman just ignored everything she said, waving her hand in the air saying, "Oh my, yes, of course you do! We'll get you all better in no time." Rolling her eyes with a sigh, Kat was too exhausted to argue for now. To the house they went with angry Jo trailing behind.

Standing before them was a very rustic three-story old farmhouse. In dire need of what used to be white paint but was now a roughened gray. Walking onto the full-length porch told of creaking boards in desperate need of replacement. The front door squealed upon opening as if the old rusty hinges were begging for a drink of oil. The feeling of a past world washed over Kat as she entered the foyer. The inside of the house was very well kept and smelled of fresh flowers and soap. The woodwork trim was that of a talented wood carver. The drapes in the windows were all lace trimmed and of a once pricey velvet. The staircase was extravagantly curved with the same carvings on the handrails. In her mind, Kat was in awe of the wealthy mansion this old farmhouse had been a very long time ago.

"Well, here we are. You can call me Miss Mam as all the others do." She turned towards the lengthy hall, and gave a call-out "Cara, dear?" Glancing back at Kat, she said, "My boys just call me Ma. Oh goodness, I haven't even gotten your name!"

Kat, realizing she was clearly getting nowhere with this woman, decided to try again anyway. "It's Katherine Forrester, but ma'am, I mean Miss Mam, could I please just use your phone? My friend Kyra will come and get me right now. I promise. You don't need to feed me or give me a room. All I want to do is go home."

Miss Mam looked puzzled and nonchalantly stated, "Oh, honey, we don't have phones around here. There simply aren't any wires."

A knot started reforming in Kat's gut. With pleading eyes, she asked, "Can you take me to the nearest one?" Miss Mam only shook her head back and forth as if sorry for the girl. Miss Mam turned back to Cara who was now standing beside her. Gesturing with her hand toward a thin pale woman with freckles and a short mop of fiery red hair.

"This is Cara…." Waving her arm back toward Kat, "And this is Katherine. She will be staying with us. She will need a nice hot bath, some fresh clothes, and a room." Miss Mam gave Kat a little guided push toward the woman. Cara gave Kat a polite nod and without saying anything reached out and took her hand, leading her up the stairs. Miss Mam turned to Jo who was hanging back toward the door. With a firm look of disapproval, she said, "I trust you will have everything in order?" Jo nodded in agreement and went back out the door.

Miss Mam waited 'til all was quiet upstairs where her boarders slept in four of the six bedrooms. Then checking with her boys Jo and Billy, all was good for the night, she went to her room on the main floor. Jo kept his room in the cellar while Pudge slept in a room next to hers.

Captain Lenard Hurrtz, an older burly man in his sixties, is a local native of the rural town of Lexville that became a great asset to the area's law enforcement. "Hey, Tad, you got a minute?"

Detective Tad Billings, average build with dark skin and hair looks straight out of *GQ Magazine* said, "Sure."

Lenny sat down and pulled out a chair for Tad in the conference room. Flipping through the missing persons papers, he said, "We have people coming up missing, Tad, I can't figure out the reasoning. I figured you coming from a bigger city, you might see something I'm not."

"Yeah, Len," Tad said, "I'll check it out. How many? Anyone I know?"

Lenny said, "Depends how far back you go. I can't believe we didn't catch this sooner. Going back five years, it's been ten total all spread out."

Tad shifted in his chair. "What's the latest?"

Eyebrows furrowed, Lenny looked up at Tad and replied, "Last night on Halloween."

Tad's stomach did a churn of nausea. "Don't tell me a kid got taken trick or treating."

"NO! Thank God, I'd have every parent in here screaming at me! Jesus, no!"

Relaxing a bit in their chairs, Tad put his hands out in question, "Girls?"

"Yes and men. These are grown people. And it's like they just up and walked off. No trace. No witnesses. Like they went on their own. Only reason anyone knew was it's all homeless people that the Free Church feeds and houses."

"They do a head count?" Tad asked.

"Yeah, every night. I got dates on every one of these people." Lenny shook his head. "Last night is the stopper."

Puzzled, Tad shifted again. "What's different?"

"She wasn't homeless."

"Who was it?"

"That cute lil gal that works over there at the law office. Friend said she never showed for their Halloween party and tried her cell."

"Wow, odd. Anyone check her residence?"

"Yeah, friend said she went there. Has her own key. No sign of her."

They stood up, and Tad grabbed up the papers and gave them a shove into the file folders. "I'll go over and make sure she's not there. Could have come in late from a date. Anyone check with her coworkers?"

"Yeah, we checked. I'll get you a key for the apartment, and yes, check with her place of work again. Thanks, Tad." Lenny pushed in their chairs as Tad nodded.

"All right. I'll take a look at it and see what I can make of it." Mumbling to himself, he added, "Isn't that a damn shame? No one noticed until a respected working citizen comes up missing. He shook his head as he went to his own office.

Miss Mam was up at the first hint of dawn preparing breakfast for all of her boarders she likes to call them. Jo appeared around the corner of the kitchen where Ma was working at the wood cook stove. Turning to see who entered,

Ma gave Jo that look again, "I trust last night will never happen again?"

Staring back into deep cold eyes of the mother he knew all too well did not take mistakes kindly when it came to her business, Jo said, "No, Ma, I will make sure it does not."

"All right then, I am quite sure you will make sure Billy"—as Ma liked to call the younger and smaller of her boys—"or yourself, is out there guarding our business night and day from here on."

"Yes, Mam." Changing her tone to the loving lady of the house, she added, "Now go make sure everyone is up and coming down for breakfast." At his hesitation, she said, "And, Jo, Have Cara get our new guest up as well. We need to get her started on her duties today." A pause, with a satisfied half smile, Ma continued, "And make sure she is FIT for her duties please."

"Yes, Mam," Jo said with a knowing grin before heading up the stairs, feeling a reprieve from the previous day's events.

Kat was pretty sure she hadn't slept a wink. Her body ached all over and her head was pounding. So much stress from the night before and now the uncertainty of what will happen today. Thinking out loud, she softly said, "Does this Miss Mam even know I was abducted by her goons? I should have gotten the heck out of here last night." Kat knew in the back of her mind that may be more difficult than she would like. Putting her hand to her throat, holding it as if for protection from an unknown evil, she gasped, "They abducted me" as reality sank in deep. Kat jumped with a jolt as the door to her room swung open.

Cara stood in the doorway staring at Kat as if she knew exactly what she was feeling. Kat just stared back at the woman with serious eyes, not knowing what to expect. "We need to get you dressed for breakfast. I will help you." Cara held out her hand. "Come on now, we gotta hurry a little. Miss Mam don't care to have people late for the meal." Kat rolled off the bed slowly and followed Cara, cautiously looking behind and to both sides as she followed her to a bathing room. This redhaired woman seemed nice enough as she laid out clean linens and a fresh scented bar of soap.

Kat reminded the woman, " I just had a bath last night."

"One cannot have too many baths around here," Cara explained. "Now strip down and climb in while I go fetch you some appropriate clothing."

Kat did what she was told. With a sigh of relief as she stepped into the warm bath, it took away all the soreness from frightful tension and manhandling. Washing vigorously, realizing it will take more of these baths to get rid of the feeling of disgust from those goon's grimy hands. Tears started to flow as the whatifs started flashing in her head. Just imagining how much worse it could have been if she hadn't escaped that shed and been brought to the house where there are people that seem to care.

Kat ducked into the bath water upon reflex as the door squeaked open and Cara re-entered the room. "I'm so sorry," she said with genuine care. "I didn't mean to scare you."

"I guess I may be a little jumpy after the ordeal last night." Kat pulled herself out of the tub as Cara stood holding out her towel and a plain linen dress and a pair of high stockings and slip-on shoes.

Cara looked at the clothing while stating, "This will be appropriate for the meal. We will change for our chores." With confusion Kat stared at Cara. "Don't you worry about it now. We need to get downstairs for breakfast and then we'll figure that all out." With that, Cara waited while Kat dressed and they quickly went downstairs to the kitchen. Cara announced their readiness as a shorter than herself woman with brown hair pulled back into a bun and cook's apron on looked up at Kat as if she'd always been there.

"Grab that other pot on the stove, please." Kat looked at Cara for approval.

"Go ahead sweetie, I'll be right behind you." Kat looked around at the massive kitchen with its cast iron cookstove powered with burning wood, large heavy utility sink and ample cupboards and counters that look as though they've been handmade. In awe, as she grabbed the pot off the stove with old towels for heat pads, Kat pictured somewhere deep in thought how the house maids must have prepared meals for all of the farmhands and family. With the long mess table set, all but Kat sat down to breakfast. Cara patted the chair next to her as an unspoken gesture to be seated. Kat complied.

Looking at everyone at the table was sort of strange how they all just went about their business as if nothing happened last night. No explanations or even apologies. They were simply starting their day. Now feeling furious, Kat pushed back her chair and stood staring at Jo.

"He abducted me last night and you all just sit there acting like nothing happened!" she shouted. Pointing towards his accomplice, "And him too! What is going on here? Why won't anyone listen to me?" Everyone at the table stared at Kat like they truly did not understand.

Miss Mam stood, putting her arm around Kat's shoulder as she spoke softly, "Now now, Miss Katherine, we know you've been through a lot. How about you get some hot biscuits and honey in your belly, then we'll take our coffee into the sitting room and discus all of that."

Miss Mam gently guided Kat back into her chair and Cara filled the empty plate in front of her, whispering, "You need to eat something. It will be a long hard day if you don't. I will be at your side. I will help you." With that, Kat glanced around the table as they all stared at their plates and chewed their food thoughtfully. Kat ate biscuits and oats realizing she hadn't much to eat yesterday. Dinner was going to be served at the Halloween party she was attending with her friends and coworkers. Tears started to creep down her cheek as she thought of her best friend Kyra who would be frantic by this morning, not knowing what happened to her.

Interrupting Kats thoughts, Miss Mam spoke with care. "I think maybe our new guest may feel a little more at home if we all just stand one at a time and introduce ourselves to this fine young lady." It started with Cara on her immediate left and on down the table. "You've met me," Cara said, putting her hand upon her chest gracefully, "Cara. I take care of the inside of the manor, smiling and re-seated.

The plump brown-haired lady stood. "I am Darci. I help Miss Mam in the kitchen."

The thirtysomething black man stood with a very honest smile. "Sam. I am very pleased to have you here. I take care of the maintenance in this beautiful estate."

Then the elderly gentleman with grayed long hair pulled back tight in a ponytail stood halfway, not making eye contact, said, "Harry here, I take care of the gardens and the yards." With a nod, he returned to his seat.

Jo stood with a very stern, manipulating stare. "You've met me. I take care of the barn, and Miss Mam is my mother." Kat stared right back as if to say, *I'll get my way soon*. Next seated to Jo's left was a pudgy plump man with dark blondish hair, the other goon that helped grab her. Standing, he stared into Kat's eyes like a hungry lion licking its chops after a filling meal.

"Just call me Pudge. Everyone but my mother here does." Still grinning with evil content, he added, "I take very good care of the animals."

Miss Mam sighed a relieved and polite smile. "Well, all is well. Let us finish and get to our daily deeds."

Tad Billings was a detective "over the hill" they liked to joke. Coming from San Francisco, California, he was used to the banter of coming over the mountain to the real side of the world. California side, they would say, is the world of fantasy.

Here crime isn't the only thing they do all day. Eating donuts and drinking coffee is a luxury. Making the change was a promise to himself to slow down a bit and breathe. Turning the key in the lock of the young lady's apartment after a few loud knocks was always a bit risky. Going in when someone was in the shower is never a good thing, as he had experienced in the past.

Upon opening the door, he gave a shout out and as he expected, no answer. After an extensive search, the detective found no evidence of foul play in the home. Looking at photos displayed, was a telltale sign that this young lady had no one close aside from the other gal in the photos. A cutesy beanpole alongside an above average beauty with oh so wonderful curves! In Tad's mind it was not hard to imagine this one being taken. In fact, his worry to that ever-sweet smile from this young lady could bring any man begging at their knees. Including himself. Tad finished up and locked up after leaving a note on the table inside the door to please call the police station upon returning home. With a sincere thank you and signed Detective Billings. Tad headed out and hit the beat joining other officers as they walked up and down the streets knocking on doors.

Kat grabbed on to Cara's arm as they departed the dining room. "I thought something was going to be done with my situation?"

Cara turned with a regretful, knowing look, whispering, "You need to hush about all that. You are here now. This is all I can do. But you have to quiet. Jo doesn't take kindly to people who seem ungrateful."

Katherine could feel the bile and anger rising again. "GRATEFUL!! I just want to go home and to work. There are people who will be worried."

Cara sighed. "Everyone has a story that never admits to being without a place. They all want everyone to believe they actually have a home where people care. I know, I used to be the same, but you have to calm down and do what he says. Fighting him will only make it worse." With caring eyes Cara walked away as Jo came up behind Kat, taking a firm hold on her arm.

"Come with me." He gave Kat a serious glare. "Keep your mouth shut or I'll gag you." Kat tried to pull away, but he just squeezed her arm tighter. This beast of a man dragged her along like a rag doll.

"Where are—?"

"I said shut your mouth." He jerked her arm harder. Kat quieted as she remembered what Cara had said. He is a very dangerous man. He took her to the back of the kitchen, to a door that was locked. "Watch your step. I don't need you to be laid up with a broken leg."

Kat rolled her eyes. "Like you'd really care." He turned and stared so deep into her being that shear fright buckled her knees. As she started to collapse on the stairs to the musty cold cellar, Jo picked her up and threw her over his burly shoulder. Knocking the wind out of her, she gasped to breathe until he finally dropped her onto the hard floor. So scared now, Kat began to shake.

Kyra entered the big square brick building that usually gave a feeling of protection, but under these circumstances, it was just dread. The sign on the front read Lexville Police. The officers were sitting at their desks all looking up at Kyra as she entered as if she were some poor girl who lost her way. "Can anyone give me an update on the missing girl?"

They just stared at her until a tall burly man approached from the room that said Captain on the door. "No news yet, young lady, but I have my best detective on it. Why don't you give me your name and number again and I'll give you a call as soon as we locate her. Katherine Forrester, correct?"

"Yes, sir, I am so worried." Feeling like a fool as tears started running down her cheek, Kyra wiped them across her hand, as a nice lady from the front desk handed her a tissue.

"Don't you worry about it, missy, if anyone can find her it will be Detective Billings." Putting her arm around Kyra and guiding her to a chair, she added, "Captain I am going to sit with this young lady and have a chat." Captain Hurrtz nodded with approval and returned to his office.

Kyra softly spoke avoiding eye contact with the nice lady. "I feel like it's my fault." Sobbing now, "I was going to pick her up for the party, but she said she wanted to walk to hand out candy on the way."

The lady sighed with understanding. "You can't blame yourself. People walk all over town here and do not come up missing. It's just one of those freak things that happens. But I assure you, these gentlemen"—she stretched her arm out, gesturing to the officers sitting at computers and on the phones—"are all working on your friend's disappearance. They won't even be going home tonight until they figure this out." She smiled sincerely as she lightly tapped the girl's back. Standing and saying thank you to them all, Kyra left and headed over to Katherine's apartment where she decided to stay until she was found, just in case she showed up. Both her and Kat had no family left, so they were each other's only family. Kyra sat staring out Kat's window, crying and wondering what she would do if she lost her best friend.

Officers on the night shift were ordered to keep working the case, so Tad went home to take a nap. He opened the door to his small apartment that evening, on main street where he lived alone. Never meeting anyone to date that didn't have a problem with his detective work, Tad spent long hours working on cold cases for the department. He threw down the files on the coffee table and went to the kitchen to grab a cup of coffee. Then he sat on his old rumpled couch and looked at the stack of files. *Sixteen people and they just now notice?*

Mumbling, "Damn. What is wrong with this!" Shame spread

over him. "They didn't notice a problem until a working woman with a place to live came up missing. What a crying shame. And it hasn't even been a whole twenty-four hours!" He let out a sigh and started reading the files. After eating his dinner, Tad walked to his window and could see the station down the street with its light on and the bustling around as their men worked. On into the night, even himself would not sleep.

Lenny went home exhausted after a long day. His wife Sharry was in the kitchen dishing up some food from dinner. "Want a glass of wine, Len? I'm having one." Lenny glanced toward the kitchen and hollered "Sure." Sharry came into the room carrying a tray of food and two glasses of pinot noir, Len's favorite. She plopped down next to Len on the firm sofa that gave Lenny a little jolt from the cushion. Looking at his not-so-graceful wife of many years, Len gave a playful grin as he thanked her for the wake up!

"Oh, and I'm very glad you did not hand me that wine!" Sharry handed him his glass of wine with a sarcastic smile and a quick peck on the cheek.

"Long day?"

"Yeah." Len rolled his eyes and stated, "A lot of domestics and now more missing persons!" With a sigh he sipped at his wine and picked at the food on the tray.

"Well, I hope I don't have to stay in the house from now on."

Len glanced her way and shook his head side to side. "Me too" He picked up his phone and hit the number 1 on speed dial that connected to his number-one detective. "Lenny here, any leads today?"

"Just an old green Buick that was seen cruising around slow while the kids were trick or treating. Neighborhood watch picked up on it. At first thinking parents following their kids door to door. But Old Lady Crawford said it was two men. And she said she knows all of the parents in the area."

Lenny sighed. "Yeah, she used to be a teacher. Follow up on it in the morning." Lenny hung up and plopped on the couch 'til he fell asleep.

Kat lay curled on her side naked and shamed, sobbing to herself as the beast redressed. He picked up his knife and grabbed her wrist, jerking it so the long metal leash would reach the heavy metal ring that was bolted to the wall. Now gagged; and her spirit broken, after hours of brutal rape, Kat hurt in all of her private places. Being a virgin made it so much worse. Not only did he take her innocence but her dignity as well. Her plans to save herself for a deep love and marriage were all taken from her. In her eyes, she may as well have died.

The hard labor of push-ups on the cold concrete floor in between episodes of horrific sex left her broken and begging for mercy. Jo went up the stairs and turned out the lights. All Kat could hear was the turn of the lock that surged dread and hatred through her whole being.

The night was silent. The only noise coming from the big grand farmhouse was the hum of the generator and Kat's quiet whimpering.

Tad walked into the musty office and laid the file folder his captain had given him onto his desk. After checking in with the other officers, Tad went to the captain's office where Lenny Hurrtz was on the phone with the FBI. He motioned his hand to the chair in front of the desk as he listened to the bantering on the other end of the line. Tad waited while he sipped his coffee and watched on as his boss took severe punishment through the phone receiver. Lenny hung up and sat back in his chair rolling his eyes and giving a sigh.

"They're sending an agent over to assist on the case. I just got an earful on why we did not let them know we had a serious problem with the missing." Tad shrugged his shoulders and agreed it should not have taken one respected citizen missing to get them to delve into the case. Lenny shook his head. "You are absolutely right. And that is why I want you to stay on the case and keep the FBI agent Carson Kratz up to speed on any leads you get."

Tad nodded. "Will do."

Lenny stood up and opened his office door. "Jack! Come in here, please." Officer Jackson Burns entered as Captain Hurrtz assigned him to personally assist Detective Billings alongside the FBI's Agent Kratz with this case. Looking at the two, he said, "Urgency is recommended to get this girl home and get the FBI off my door step!"

"I've got a couple leads to act on. There were a few vehicles unidentified that night. And Shirley Powers says she heard a brief screech. She figured it was just the kids running around scaring people, but looked out her window anyway to see a car peel away. All she could identify was a green car."

Lenny nodded. "That's two strikes on a green car." The men shook hands and left.

Tad had Jack retrace Katherine's walk from her apartment to the address of the party, even though he'd already followed it several times. Rechecking in with residents that have a clear view of the street that may not have been home earlier. Tad met with Agent Kratz back at the precinct. Kratz brought all files that pertain to other missing homeless or young women in surrounding areas. They spent the rest of the day and night combing over all related cases.

Kyra dragged her tired body out of bed and called into work for the third day in a row. She just couldn't go on with life back to normal until her dearest friend in the whole world was found. Still carrying around that pit of dread in the bottom of her gut that she could be dead, was weighing heavy on her health. Not sleeping or eating much was finding her back in bed each day. At least putting coffee on and sticking bread into the toaster was a huge improvement. As the coffeepot burped someone knocked on the door. Kyra jumped, and collected her courage as she opened the door. A rather tall and quite good-looking officer was standing in front of her. Kyra gasped with her hand to her mouth. Not quite sure if his overwhelming good looks were the cause, or the panic of possibly bad news.

"Mam, I'm sorry to scare you, but are you Katherine Forrester?" Kyra looked at the officer puzzled.

"No, I'm Kyra Banks, her best friend. Please tell me you haven't found her body somewhere." Wet tears started to gather in her eyes.

"Ma'am—?"

She quickly cut in, "It's Kyra, please. I'm so sorry. I'm just so worried I can hardly breathe."

The officer started again, "Kyra … I am Officer Jack Burns of the Lexville Police. I'm just checking in to see if the young lady Katherine has returned yet."

Kyra opened the door wider and motioned for him to enter. "I've been staying here 24/7 for that reason," she explained, sighing. "I keep hoping she'll will come through that door or at least call me." Officer Burns politely remained standing as Kyra plopped down on the couch with her head in her hands. "I don't know what to do," Kyra exclaimed as she raised her eyes to the officer before her.

"Ma'am, you are doing exactly what we need you to do. Please stay here and contact us immediately if you hear anything." He reached out his hand and politely laid his card on the coffee table in front of her. Kyra put her hand on the card lightly, and hesitated, as if it would bring her home.

She looked up with pleading eyes. "Please find her." Jack nodded and turned for the door and left quietly. Kyra put her hand over her face and wept.

Miss Mam, happily singing to herself, was busy in the kitchen baking rolls for dinner and cake for their new member of the family. "Cara! are you close?" Cara came into the kitchen in her scrubs and gloves, "Yes, Mam, I am. What would you like me to do?"

"Oh dear, could you please make sure Miss Katherine's room is nice and clean and warmed up? I want her to be nice and warm tonight."

With a curtsy and a warm smile, Cara replied, " I would love to!" She smiled and hurried up the stairs.

"Darci darling, would you mind making the prettiest and sweetest icing for Katherine's cake?" Cheerily moving about the kitchen, Miss Mam put a little skip in her step as well. She busily went back to her deeds, then turned to Darci. "Isn't it going to be a splendid evening?"

Darci looked up from her cooking and smiled gratefully. "Yes, Mam, it is." Back to work, the ladies of the house tended their duties. Jo was out at the barn when Pudge came in the back door. He attempted a hand on the cellar door when Miss Mam turned around and swung her wooden spoon at him. "Billy Jud Baur. You stay away from that door!"

Billy looked at Ma seriously. "Why does Jo get to do all the teaching around here?" He stood his ground as Miss Mam seared his eyes with her own like a dragon's fire. He stepped back a few steps and nodded his surrender, backing his way out the door and stomped all the way back to the barn. Miss Mam turned to Darci with a nod and Darci returned hers with a grateful smile.

Jo was just finishing up with the butchering of meat for the grand dinner this evening when Pudge came through the door with a rebellious snort. Jo stared his brother down in a way that put his little brother back where he belonged. Billy said nothing and started hauling unwanted pieces of bone to the burning barrels out back. Then threw the other scraps to the pigs as they scurried about squealing at each other.

Jo headed for the house and went straight to the cellar where he enjoyed the privacy of his own space. He went over to Kat who was curled up with nothing but a blanket over her and stared down at her. Kat surrendered her eyes to the floor and begged for him quietly to please leave her alone.

Jo went into the bath and cleaned up. Before dressing he returned to Kat's side. Still chained to the wall but able to reach the bed, she lay in wait as she knew he was not done with her yet. Tears did not come anymore as he abruptly entered her. She just lay out and let him do what he wanted while she patiently waited for him to finish. Then he released her hand from the wall and carried her to the wash tub and rinsed her off and helped her with her clothes. Uncaring and brutish like his sex.

Kat didn't fight or argue. She followed him up the stairs and he guided her up the next set of stairs to her room. They came in as Cara waited for her as if she knew exactly when she would arrive, delivered by the same manly beast that Cara and probably Darci as well, all suffered the same "training," as he called it. Cara stepped forward reaching out for Kat's hand as she nodded obedience to the man beast as he was. Jo turned and left. Kat just stood there in total surrender, knowing also that she, this Cara woman, knew exactly what went on down there in the cellar.

Cara handled her keep as gently as she could and whispered to Kat softly as she took her to the bathing room and washed her so gently in all the places the beast had been and touched. "Nice warm water for my lady." Cara cooed her and brushed her hair with soft bristles. "We'll make you so pretty for your coming out party!" Excited but still gentle and soothing, Cara used lavender-scented soap all over her body and throughout her hair and gave her motherly kisses on the forehead as she helped her out of the tub. Patting her dry, she brought out a beautiful dress of blue satin and silver lace to do up her hair.

When Cara was finished, she pulled Kat over to the full-length mirror and smiled ear to ear at her as she turned her around in the reflection like a delicate china doll. Kat finally looked into Cara's eyes and whispered. "Thank you." Cara gave a quick kiss on her cheek and quickly changed from her cleaning scrubs and also put on a pretty dress and they went down the stairs to make a grand entrance. All were waiting for the re-entrance of the ladies with waltz music playing and all were dressed for the occasion. Miss Mam jumped with glee as they entered the room. Cara paraded Katherine through the receiving line and curtsied to each family member as they made their way to the dining room.

Miss Mam smiling from ear to ear as well, said, "Oh my beautiful darling girl! Look how perfectly scrumptious you are! And look at this delicious cake your sister Darci decorated for you!" Miss Mam went around the table pulling out chairs as everyone sat down. The table was filled with food like Thanksgiving dinner. They all filled their plates as Darci went around with the tea and coffee. She, too, was dressed for a party and Miss Mam looked elegant. Kat slowly glanced around the table as everyone bowed their heads while Miss Mam read from the book she called her bible. Kat emotionally bowed her head and to herself thanked God as it could be worse. Everyone ate and chatted of upcoming chores they could take on.

Harry and Sam discussed rebuilding the front porch while Miss Mam and Darci collected the dishes and headed to the kitchen hen pecking all the way. Jo and Pudge stepped outside to smoke a cigar and Cara took Kat's hand and pulled her to the front hall where the music was beaming out. She led Kat into a waltz and cooed her some more as they waltzed through the room. Kat stepped on Cara's toe and laughter spilled out like a balloon losing its air. The more the two laughed the louder Kat bellowed. Releasing all the pent-up emotion her laughter turned to tears. Cara shushed the tears wiping her new friend and sister's face and kissed her again, only this time on the lips. They both returned to laughter and kept on dancing. Soon Darci had entered the room pulling Miss Mam behind her as they joined the waltz, flinging their aprons off and singing silly songs.

Jo stepped in and watched as his women enjoyed the party. Billy left for town to carouse and Sam politely stepped in to waltz Kat around the room as Harry took Cara in his arms.

"Ah What a splendid evening it's been!" Miss Mam sang out as she passed the ladies on the dance floor.

Morning came quick for Detective Billings. Falling asleep at his desk did not bode well for his kinked-up spine. Stretching and rubbing his head was all he could manage until Agent Kratz set a fresh hot cup of coffee in front of him. "Oh man, you know how to please a man! Too bad you're not a young, gorgeous female!"

Eyes wide awake and eyebrows elevated, "I, Agent K, have been busy while you slumped over lazily like a baby!"

"Yeah?" Tad replied.

"Yes, sir, my dear man. And please call me Carson."

"We spent the night together, I suppose, first name basis would be appropriate! Call me Tad."

"Now that we have that settled, I found, not four, but six related cases in the surrounding counties. One in Jasper, two in Schooner, and one in Kaleva," Agent Kratz said. "And two more witnesses that saw a big green car!"

"Wow, I'd say donuts for all! That is fantastic."

"Let's hit the beat in those counties, see what pops up." Both men grabbed their coffees and headed out, stopping at the captain's office door to give him the information and plan for the day.

Breakfast went quick at the grand manor as everyone was tired from the party last evening. Cara in her scrubs, Miss Mam and Darci in their kitchen clothes, and Kat was given scrubs as well. It was decided that Cara could sure use help with scrubbing floors. The men nodded politely as they waited and watched until the ladies all passed to tend to their chores. Then Sam and Harry went out to measure the front porch for supplies. Jo motioned for Pudge to go to the barn without him. Then followed Kat to the utility room where the cleaning supplies were kept. Kat felt his presence under her skin and turned her head just enough to catch the beast in her peripheral vision. Jo kept some distance but didn't let his new woman out of his sight.

Cara turned to Kat when she realized Jo was stalking them and whispered, "Just stay close, the sooner we get to our chores the better." Jo did not leave them alone until Pudge summoned Jo to the barn. Kat let out a long sigh of relief, to have the beast away for a bit.

Pudge turned up the only source of outside communication that consisted of a small battery-operated AM radio. A local report was put out for any information on a missing twenty-two-year-old woman from Lexville. They also put out an alert for information on any large older green cars, possibly Buicks. Jo angered, as no one has ever cared or looked for the people they'd brought to the farm before. But in reality, they both new this woman was different and they would surely wreak hell upon them for it.

"Fuck, Jo. I don't want to get caught with this bitch here. She ain't worth all that."

Jo, disgusted with his brothers whining, turned and punched Pudge in the head, knocking him down as he warned through gritted teeth, "I told you when you saw her to let it go. You little bastard. You're the one who jumped out of the car and grabbed her. We should have taken her straight to the barn."

Pudge scooted away weakly from his dangerous older brother, and stayed on the ground until Jo stormed off. Then he watched his brother grab the can of gas and went out the back behind the barn. Pudge followed keeping his distance. Jo yelled, "Get in" as he opened the door of the green Buick they used to go to town for supplies. Pudge did what he was told and they drove out to the field away from the house. Jo took everything they needed from the car and then poured gasoline inside and out. Then he pulled out his lighter from his pocket and threw it in the car. Pudge jumped from the car as it went up in flames afraid for his life.

Jo stared into his brother's eyes and said, "Ever put us in this position again and I will kill you." Pudge knew his brother well, all the way to the pit of hell he called his gut. He kept his distance and did what he was told. Jo called out in command, "Go get the truck." Pudge drove the old pickup truck they used to haul hay, around to the back of the barn. Jo looked at his brother and said, "Tune it up, and take that old plate off the back and make that your job until its road ready. I don't want to see you at the dinner table or the kitchen until that's done. This truck better be road ready by tomorrow morning." With that, Jo headed back to the house.

With each day that passed with Katherine still missing, Kyra was accepting the fact that she may never see her friend again. She tidied up Kat's apartment with emotional bouts, and packed up her things to move back to her own place. She just couldn't stay there any longer without losing her mind. Kyra picked up the card the officer left, and left a message that she will be at her own residence, or her work, if he needs her. Then with a tear rolling down her cheek, she closed and locked Kat's door.

Officer Jack Burns checked his messages, listening to Kyra's message, he felt a bit of understanding, and went to make sure the missing gal's apartment was secure.

Captain Lenny Hurrtz called a meeting with Agent Kratz,

his number-one detective, Tad, and Officer Jack Burns. They brought all of their leads and findings together and formed a task force to go checking in rural areas for any sign of the alleged green car or the description of the missing girl. Lenny had a crowd of officers and volunteers in the office as he handed out the descriptions.

"It's been too long people! I want businesses, residents, and rural areas approached. We need to give this case closure. If we find Katherine Forrester, I'm quite confident we will put to rest the case of the homeless disappearances. Miss Forrester was last seen wearing her Halloween costume as a homeless beggar. You already have all that info in your hand. We keep coming up with dead ends on this. Get out there and find this young lady." They all grabbed coffees and donuts for the road and spread out into the surrounding counties.

Miss Mam called out to the men to come in for lunch. Harry and Sam dropped their duties and helped get food on the table with eagerness from hungry bellies. "Harry dear, would you please go fetch Jo and Billy for the meal?" Harry being a quiet sort, gave a nod of welcome acknowledgment. Harry was the only other family member that was allowed to approach the barn. A large cow bell hung on the outside wall next to the barn door. Harry would ring the bell twice for meal times, three times for Miss Mam's summons and continuous for emergencies. No one was ever allowed into the barn. Harry and Sam knew they were to never speak of others who tried and were taken away.

Cara and Kat went upstairs to change for the midday meal. None of the boarders were allowed to the dinner table in filth, as Miss Mam called it. The bathing rooms were filled with fresh warm water by Cara and Kat for washing before meals. Fresh clothes were set out for each member of the manor and their working clothes were then hung for after the meal. This made Cara and Kat the last of the boarders to the kitchen. Jo came in through the back kitchen door in a rush calling out orders to the men to guard the upstairs.

"NOW!"

Sam piped up a "yes, sir" and Harry nodded and followed as they ran up the steps. The ladies were at the top of the stairs when they all heard a loud banging on the front door. Miss Mam calmly came from the kitchen while Miss Darci stayed back. Jo gave Ma a serious look and she nodded agreement as she collected herself to open the door. Sam and Harry pushed the ladies back to their rooms and held them there. Kat felt a feeling of panic.

She looked at Harry with pleading eyes and her hand at her mouth. "It could be someone looking for me!" She gasped as Jo appeared behind Harry.

"Harry, go downstairs in case Ma needs you," he ordered, all the while keeping piercing eyes on Kat. "Not a word," he told her." As Jo forced a firm hand over Kat's mouth. Kat whimpered and felt her knees buckle as she fell to the floor. Jo shoved her out of the way with his boot and quietly closed her door.

Miss Mam kept her composure just fine and answered the officer's questions. "I'm so sorry I couldn't be of more help, sir, I just haven't seen anyone around here like that." The officer nodded a thank you and left his card. Jo waited until the police cruiser crept down the two-track slowly and out of sight before he grabbed Kat's arms and yanked her to her feet. She was devastated to have someone come for her and she was trapped and silenced.

She hit at the beast of a man with her fists and yelled, "I hate you, I just want to kill you, you dirty pig!" Jo dragged her as she swung her fists all the way to the cellar.

The rest of the family of boarders ate in solemn silence. As they all knew the fate of their newest sister. So many had come and gone over time that did not comply to the family rules. Jo did not come back upstairs.

Evenings came early on the farm as Miss Mam slipped about the quiet manor blowing out lanterns and candles. It was early to bed and early to rise. Everyone goes to their rooms at nightfall. There is no electricity, so natural ways are used. Miss Mam stopped at the cellar door off the kitchen as a quiet whimpering came from below. With motherly correction, Miss Mam cooed through the closed door, "Shoosh now, child. You only brought this on yourself. Sleep now." Miss Mam blew out the kitchen light and went to her room.

The next three days went quickly, as Kyra returned to her job at the grocery store, and that sweet officer, Jack, had checked on her a couple of times. Smiling for the first time since Kat went missing, she reveled in the much-needed attention. Kyra now looked forward to something again. She went back to her paperwork in the back office when she looked up to see that very attractive officer Mr. Jack Burns leaning against the wall watching her. Kyra smiled as he entered the office and displayed a Royal Prince as he bent down and took her hand to his lips and gently kissed it. An overwhelming warmth and sexual energy went through her whole being, and she thought she would faint!

"Officer Burns! You're melting me like warm honey!" Jack smiled and bowed as he let go of her hand. "Do you bring any news?" Ky raised her hopeful brows.

"I am sorry to say no but am very hopeful you will accept my invitation to dinner tonight." He waited patiently as Ky curtsied and smiled a definite yes. "Pick you up at 7?"

"That sounds absolutely wonderful!" Jack did a professional about face and marched out the door. Kyra giggled and went back to work hoping to finish and cut out early so she could primp a little for her date.

Lenny Hurrtz assigned a group of volunteers to stay through the night to read over and organize the days beat results. He stopped off at the gas station before heading home and noticed a short plump guy smoking a cigarette while he was pumping gas. "Hey! Put that cigarette out!" The man looked at Lenny and realized he was driving a police-marked car.

"Shit" The plump man looked a little frazzled and hurried on out.

Lenny shook his head and mumbled, "Dumb ass." Lenny got home and plopped on the couch. He leaned back and sighed. Sharry, by routine, brought him wine and dinner, knowing until this big case was solved, Len would eat, drink, and sleep on that couch. Being married for many years, she really didn't mind at all. It really wasn't very often they would get a case big as this in their little town.

Tad stretched out on the sofa at the precinct to take a nap. His desk was not good rest. Maybe tomorrow they would get some descent leads. A coworker walked by and flipped off the light as Tad was already snoring.

Agent Kratz went to his hotel room to catch some shut-eye as well. All in all, they brought in a lot of information today. Now they can hope the night crew can find some similarities. Carson, too, was out in minutes.

Kyra rushed home to change for her date. Jack came promptly at seven and they headed out on foot hand in hand, talking about work and family and dreams. "The only thing that would make me happier right now is if my best friend were back home safe and sound."

Jack put his arm around Ky's shoulder and gave a warm squeeze. Before they went into the restaurant Ky looked up and said, "Would you mind if we just went to the pub and got some burgers and a beer?"

Jack looked surprised. "Uh, sure, why not? I like a burger

and beer! But do note your royal prince was taking you to a nice romantic restaurant!"

Ky smiled and answered, "Duly checked!" So they walked a little farther and Ky heard a ringtone play. She stopped in her tracks and looked at Jack quite strangely.

"What's wrong?"

Ky put her hand to her mouth and gasped a little. "How many cell phones have you heard that play that goofy tune?"

Jack tilted his head and listened closely. "I have to say I have never heard that."

Ky said with satisfaction, "Exactly!" Holding her breath while they tried to follow the ringtone, it stopped. "Oh my God, NO! It's got to be close." They waited a few minutes and they heard it go to voicemail alert. "THERE!" Ky ran over to a residential front porch where a young boy was sitting with his friend looking at their phones.

"Hey, where did you get that phone?" Jack questioned as they walked up to the boys.

"I found it over there in the bushes."

"We didn't steal," the other boy said. "It was just there ringing." Jack took the phone and showed it to Kyra.

With dread, she said, "Oh my God, Jack, that is Kat's phone." Jack thanked the boys and they went straight to the precinct.

Lenny's phone rang on the coffee table that also vibrated itself onto the floor. He jumped out of his dead of sleep, and fished around on the floor for his phone. Picking it up quickly, he said, "Lenny here."

"Captain, this is Jack. We just found our missing girl's phone just off Main Street."

"Stay there with it. I'll be there in a minute."

Jack shouted, "Wait! We're at the station."

Lenny gave the order straight as he was rushing out the door. "Meet me at Gills Hilltop."

"Okay." Jack and Kyra left for the meet. While Lenny got on the phone to Tad and Agent Kratz. They all met and Kyra was already looking through Kat's phone for anything that might help.

It was almost morning by the time They were able to charge up Kat's phone and view photos and videos that she had taken around the time she went missing. There were many pictures of the neighborhood kids that posed in their costumes for Kat. Ky said her and Kat did some fill-in days at the elementary school for kids in summer classes last year. They got to know a lot of the children in the area. Agent Kratz plugged Kat's phone into his computer so they could zoom in better and maybe enhance some of them if needed. The detective volunteers from other areas had put together a board of organized information of all that seemed connected.

Kyra saw the board with Kat's picture pinned up and pictures of any big old green cars that were found within a fifty-mile radius as well as any info on the other missing people. The team found similarities to strangers not from the area, a couple of counties over. Two, not so nice men had been seen many times in every county around their area. Said they would come in and shop for a month's worth of groceries including women's needs. They're all describing them similar. One short and chubby, lighter hair, and the other one mean and tall with dark hair. Lenny pulled everyone out during the wee hours to start looking for these two men for questioning.

The officers were revisiting all of the rural-area residences to find anyone living in them that matched the men's descriptions. With warrants to search properties that are likely to have family members living there but may not be home. More agents were brought in from the FBI as well, now that they had possible suspects.

Kat lost track of the days, as she lay out, bruised from brutality and abuse. Not knowing as she lay there naked, hungry, and cold if she would ever be allowed to leave the musty old cellar. She couldn't remember what her life was like anymore. Everything was a blur. The beast didn't give her food for a couple days as severe punishment but was now bringing more than she could eat. Unsure why he started feeding her again, she ate anyway, just to stay alive as long as she could. She could no longer refer to this beast by name. She just knew deep inside he was the devil himself. It was so dark most of the time in the cellar. Kat could not tell if it was daytime or night. Her captor would come and go, taking his pleasures from her each time. Of course, he would rinse her off at times with cold water, then chain her back up.

Jo left the girl in the cellar for now, knowing soon he would have to get rid of her for good, he wasn't quite sure why he had kept her this long. He just knew she would be the death of them all. On their way to a city an hour away, Pudge filled Jo in on the info he'd picked up in Lexville the other night. Pudge would go on drunken bouts at the bars in the area to pick up women for his needs, and listen to the talk to take back to Jo. "You're going to quit going to town. It's too risky now. You'll go with me on supply day and that's it." Jo gave Pudge a threatening stare.

"Come on, man. I gotta go, Jo. Sides you ner let me have a turn at home."

Jo stared at the road. "I said no. Don't cross me, Billy." Pudge hit the dashboard with his fist and stared out the window in surrender. Jo turned into the back parking lot of the grocery store. "No one has seen us here. We're an hour out and have a different vehicle." Now go in and get only what's on our list." Jo shouted at his brother sitting right next to him "DO NOT TALK TO ANYONE! Understand?" Pudge gave an obedient nod and was off. Jo stayed at the truck smoking a cigarette. He watched as cars went by and people passed without looking at him. This made him confident that no one would even notice them. *It's a bigger city and the alert is looking for a green car closer to home.*

Pudge came out of the store with two carts full of supplies. Jo ordered him into the truck while he loaded. The less they are seen together the better. They went from there to the lumber yard where Jo picked up wood, nails, and everything his workers needed to fix the rotting porch. They are fine men he has for the estate. They are respectful and mind their place. Jo has been very pleased with his ladies as well. They do their chores and are obedient to him and Ma. Yes, 'til they brought that little sprite home, everything was just fine and good. Pudge was silent most of the way home, so Jo gave his brother something to look forward to.

"Soon we'll need to find a couple more boarders for Ma. She needs another woman to help Cara, and Harry is getting old. We will need to train a younger groundskeeper to help Harry until it is time for him to give. "Ah, Jo! Thanks, man. It's what I live for!"

"Yeah, well, these ones will be for Ma. We need to make sure they're trainable."

Pudge, still excited, said, "Fun, man, A brew with the bro and the thrill of the hunt!" Jo didn't smile much, but his little brother's excitement did give a little pep in his step. Jo punched the gas pedal of the old truck and let out a brief snort as Billy hooted and cheered him on.

"Nice tune-up, Pudge." With that, they enjoyed the rest of the ride home.

The next morning, Miss Mam gave Jo a questioning look as he appeared from the cellar. Jo stared back at Ma as he took a glass of juice from her. "You know that one," Jo began, glancing at the cellar door, "will be the end to us all."

Ma gave a half grin. "Well, I've noticed it's taking you a long time to decide." Jo grumbled. "You think you know this, son?" Ma started humming a cheery song as she dove into her work. "You know, Jo, your Ma may have a couple ideas that may help you!" Jo gave a knowing nod and went to the barn without breakfast meal.

Everyone ate the morning meal in quiet curiosity as Jo, their leader made no appearance. It was the first time any of them could remember him not being at a meal to keep order and control status amongst the family. No one, however, would ever step out of their place to question the Master of the house for fear of punishment. They go about their purpose and leave questions to Miss Mam and Jo.

Jo busied himself in the barn, slamming things and cussing every chance he got. Pudge had finished the meal and stayed clear of Jo unless summoned. When his older brother was in a foul mood, one just didn't get in his war path.

Jo conceded to Ma's urging of trying things her way for a day. He went to the cellar and used extreme brutality for his pleasures as a warning to his quarry that it can always be worse. When he was through with her, he took her to the wash tub. He went upstairs to get hot water off the cookstove and poured it in the tub while holding his hand over her mouth. He endured watching her gasp and tears run down her face as her lower extremities reddened. This was the first time in Jo's entire life to feel the most unwanted emotion in his chest that he was damned determined to keep from showing. He pulled her out of the tub and wrapped a blanket around her, then carried her up the stairs, for one more try of obedience. As he passed her off to Cara's care, he pulled her head back by her hair and seared a fiery warning into her eyes. Then he left the house.

Jo summoned Pudge to the barn and uncovered the underground shelter in the floor of the barn where he kept all of his weapons. Pudge jumped up and down with boyish glee. Together they armed rifles and handguns and old military bayonets. To add to Pudge's excitement Jo handed his little brother an assault rifle.

"You are my hero, man! Are we takin 'em down?"

Jo replied with absolute, "If they come for her."

Pudge hooted and held his gun to the sky. "YES, MAN!"

In the house, Miss Mam went up to Kat's room where Cara was tending the whimpering woman's scorched wounds. When Miss Mam entered, Cara gave her a pleading look. "Now let me see what we have here." Cara stepped back and Miss Mam checked her patient carefully as Kat provided fresh tears down her cheeks like a fountain. "You, my dear, must learn to never anger your master." With a soothing smile Miss Mam continued, "I am absolutely positive you are going to be just fine. We'll keep some salve on it and you'll feel better in no time." Miss Mam gave Cara instructions on the care of their patient. Cara was to stop all chore duties until she says otherwise and be the sole caretaker of Miss Katherine. Treat her as a patient, and not to lose sight of her. Cara was thankful and hugged Miss Mam. "Oh, my dear sweet girls, you are the sunshine of my heart!"

Cara tended to Kat's every need. Meals were brought up to her on trays and books were read to her at her bedside by Cara and Sam on occasion. Even Harry gifted the young lady with his presence, and told her old war stories. Katherine's need and want to go back to her life was put aside, and replaced with the unrelenting determination of her new family to keep her.

Katherine Forrester's cell phone did not lead investigators any closer to finding her, but Agent Carson Kratz sent it to the forensics lab at the FBI anyway.

With officers and agents all out combing the surrounding counties and rural areas, Captain Hurrtz carried on with some of the local, current cases, along with just a couple of patrolmen. Lenny turned from his patrolmen as he picked up his phone that had already wrung twice with new voicemails.

"Yeah? ... Hey, Sharry, I'm sorry, babe. I know. It's just been so crazy around here. Can you still cancel? Oh great! Thank you, sweetheart. I promise I'll make it up to you when this big case is finally wrapped up ... Okay, I love you too! ... Oh, hey! I'll be home late again. Sorry. bye."

Captain Hurrtz turned back to his patrolmen, apologizing for the interruption. They waved it off and snorted a laugh. "We have wives too, man, totally understand." With that, they went back to discussions on who was doing what next, to tally up some of the domestic disturbance cases they had piling up.

Detective Tad Billings nodded at the gentleman at the gas station out on Route 4, south of town, as he gave a basic description of a big Buick. "Yeah, uh, it were near a month ago or so. I was sittin' here on my stool like I do. An here come a big ole Buick station wagon of sorts, just a honkin' on that horn. That's why I notice he was in some kinda hurry out there."

"Do you remember what he looked like?" Tad asked.

"Ahhh, well, not really. Seemed kinda short behind that wheel though, in such a big car." Tad gestured for the man to continue. "He ... uh, just sat there a few minutes or so and then pulled on out. Guess he mighta thought I was a full-service station maybe. Kinda strange. But I just went on back to my customers and kinda forgot about it all 'til now. I heard yer alert on the radio here."

Tad thanked the man and started to leave and then turned back to the man briefly. "Was the car green?"

The man smiled. "Green as the grass in summer!" Tad smiled with a nod of thanks and left.

He then rang Agent K, his newfound buddy. "Hey, just talked with the gas station attendant out south of town. Sounds like it could have been our car and one of our guys driving."

Agent Kratz responded, "Well, that gives us some more area

to cover." Sounding hopeful, he added, "When you have no registration anywhere within four counties, it's frustratingly difficult to find some old green car, that could literally be anywhere!" Tad agreed and hung up. With a long sigh, Detective Tad Billings headed out south of town for a little drive. Just maybe he'd happen on a big green car.

Cara finished brushing out Katherine's hair and startled a bit when Jo swung the door open. Cara stood immediately, resembling a private at roll call. Jo gave her the down to business glare and motioned toward her patient without looking at the woman in the bed. "Can she get out of that bed yet?" He hesitated a second. "Can't imagine she's that sick. I need her up and coming down to meals." Cara looked to the floor as one would do to not challenge a ferocious grizzly.

"Yes, sir, Master Jo. I will have her up and dressed for this evening's meal." Cara still kept her eyes diverted away from his and gave an absolute nod as to not anger the beast standing but three feet from her safety. Jo attempted a half glance in Kat's direction and displayed a look of disgust. "Get her up now and I want her hair cut off and dyed red like yours."

Cara knew better than to ask how she could possibly dye Kat's hair to a bright red. She curtsied with a nod and replied as enthusiastically as she could muster, "Yes, sir. Immediately." Jo grunted as he left abruptly.

Cara regrettably pulled down the covers that were covering Miss Katherine's lower extremities, and gently applied fresh salve as she quietly explained that the Master, which Kat referred to as the Beast, needs her up and dressed for this evening's meal … *aaannd*, she will need to cut off her hair, short like hers and red.

Katherine was already tearing up as she heard everything the Beast had said. She wasn't sure if she was upset because she would lose her beautiful hair … or … because the brutality he spends on her is clearly enough to feel his hatred of her, and now he hates how she looks as well. Staring at the ceiling and trying so hard not to break down and sob, Kat swallowed and wiped the tears away with anger. Cara cooed her along as she helped her out of the bed. Kat winced a few times from the burns but succeeded at getting to the washroom. Cara opened the bedroom door and summoned Sam who was near, to go tell Miss Mam she needs something to dye Katherine's hair red. Sam looked confused, but knew better than to ever question the ladies of the house when on a mission. Off he went with seriousness.

Miss Mam was in the kitchen humming and standing over the utility basin when Sam approached with a gentle "ahem … Miss Mam."

She turned with a quizzical look, "Yes, Mr. Sam, you may speak." Always so welcoming when one's needs are approached.

"Mam, if I may. Cara will need your presence in the Lady Katherine's room, with a bit of red for dying hair?" With a gracious nod, he stood until he was properly dismissed.

"Thank you, dear Sam, I will be more than happy to hither Miss Cara's request." With a warm smile, Miss Mam touched Sam's shoulder lightly as she passed, and softly gave him dismissal.

Miss Mam smiled knowingly as she went to her washroom closet. For it was her suggestion to Jo, that he change her looks in case more visitors happen along. In her closet she stored a variety of hair colors from previous years for occasional identity changes. Bright red was a color she herself had used long ago and a little sister to Cara will be perfectly believable. No one sees a blonde or a brunette when a drastic red is standing before them and definitely no similarity to a full head of brunette. She grabbed everything needed, including an eyebrow brush, and patches for the eyes. Singing along as she entered Kat's room, Miss Mam gave the woman a light tap on the shoulder of reassurance as Cara cut long thick tresses of brown hair from her quarry's head. Tears flowed as Kat watched her beautiful hair fall. It lay on the floor like death to who she once was. Attempting a look at the reflection she did not want to see, Kat lifted her chin and knew, there was no going back now. This new person she is finding in the mirror is who she is now. The prisoner of the Beast.

Kyra stretched out on her couch hoping to hear from her handsome officer. Since their burger and beer was canceled, she had not heard from him. Trying so hard not to think of Kat and what may have happened to her, Kyra closed her eyes and was determined to be in her world now. She should not feel guilty for moving on and living her life. Feeling almost angry now for Kat doing this to her. Just then her phone rang. "Hello?"

A sexy drawled out voice said, "Is this the most beautiful woman in the world?"

Ky laughed. "Well, I would like to say of course, but that is not my job to say so."

Jack grinned on the other end. "Well, the verdict will have to be investigated, of course. So, I suggest you doll yourself up so I can take you out on a test run." Kyra giggled into the phone and hung up quick as she ran to the bath. A quick shower and some light makeup applied, Ky stood in the mirror hoping the sexy dress with black stockings wasn't overkill. She just came out of the bedroom as the buzzer went off at her door. Giggling as she opened the door, Jack was leaning against the wall with his dress shirt opened halfway down and tight black trousers with shiny shoes.

His chocolate hair was flopped lazily to one side and deep blue eyes with a grin that would melt any woman or man. She was in awe and speechless. Jack scanned over her with pleasure on his mind. "Would you like to get that burger and beer now?" Kyra gave a satisfied grin. Jack reeled her into the warmth of his chest and bestowed a lengthy kiss to lips that clearly stated a very deep connection.

Melting under Jack's hold, Kyra whispered, "I don't think I can stay on my feet long enough to get downstairs!" With a long painful groan, Jack slowly closed the door and picked Ky up and carried her, kissing her all the way to the bedroom. The apartment went dark and the sweet whispers of love and gentle love making were all that could be heard.

Kat sat quietly at the meal while staring at her plate of food. She wasn't sure if the food itself was nauseating her insides, or the fact pressing so violently against the back of her mind, that she will never escape this place. Everyone ate as if it were perfectly natural for Kat to be sporting new hair. With much zeal, Miss Mam addressed all at the dining table before leaving to clean up. "I would like to introduce our new family member!" Everyone seemed excited and all eyes were suddenly on her as Miss Mam motioned Kat to stand. Miss Mam turned her defining eyes to Cara as she introduced Cara's younger sister Sara "that has come to live with us here at our Manor Farm."

With that, everyone stood and smiled as they nodded acceptance of the alleged newcomer. Kat's heart sank in her chest and suddenly, she felt a bout of rejection deep in the pit of her stomach. Quickly turning away from the table, Kat, now Sara, heaved her fresh meal to the floor. Cara instantly wrapped her arm around Sara's shoulders in support as she guided her now, younger sister away from the trauma of her status.

Miss Mam instantly cooed, "Oh the poor dear, all of that stressful traveling to get here has rendered her ill."

Darci spoke up, looking at Cara. " Don't worry about the mess, Cara. I will take care of that if"—she turned questioning eyes to Miss Mam—"it is permissible with Miss Mam.

"Oh dear, of course. Cara you just take your sister Miss Sara on up to her room. I'm quite sure she must be exhausted. Please unpack her belongings and turn down her bedding, Cara, and we will take care of things down here." Every one instantly sprang into action to clean up dinner remnants and Darci retrieved a mop.

Cara took Sara to a different room and turned down the bedding so she could lie down. Speaking with enthusiasm but softly, as she knew her new sister was slightly unstable, she said, "I am so thankful you came, Sara. I missed you so much. And don't fret. You will love it here. Everyone is so kind and helpful." Cara looked away and paused. "There is one that you must absolutely obey at any cost. He is the Master of the Manor. His name is Jo, and you must never, ever go near the barn. Also, Miss Mam is the highest Grand Lady of the Manor. Never question her as well. Do what you are told."

Cara changed her tone back to pure excitement! "We are going to have so much fun!" Cara placed her hands on Sara's shoulders. "You are never going to want to leave here." More of a statement of fact than hope. Kat, now Sara, just stared back at Cara with complete understanding. Cara is getting the sister she so dreamed of, and everyone is excited to have her as someone else because Katherine Forrester was not liked and no longer existed. Sara looked down at her hands as if seeing them as someone else's. Then she went to the mirror and stared at the reflection until she no longer saw Katherine. It is only Sara in the mirror.

Cara came up behind her sister, putting her arms around her and gave her a very light kiss on the cheek and whispered in her ear, "You are my sister, and I love you so very much. This is what has to be. It is what's best for all." Cara went to Katherine's old room and packed up everything and took it downstairs to Miss Mam. She handed the bag of clothes and personal items, including what Kat was wearing when she arrived to the Lady of the manor with mutual understanding. Miss Mam nodded in confirmation of the deed. Cara knew what she needed to do without Miss Mam's say so. They are a true family at the manor, and everyone has the same understanding of things that need to happen to protect the family at any cost.

Detective Tad Billings sat at his kitchen table looking over pictures and interviews with possible leads. Frustrated and tired, he got up and poured himself a glass of bourbon and let out a long sigh as he took a drink. He leaned on his counter staring at a picture of Katherine May Forrester. To himself he asked with a quiet voice, "Where are you?" The picture he had was captivating. Her smile was sincere, but her eyes spoke of spunk and defiance. He grinned and spoke to the eyes of controversy.

"I would love to try my hand at figuring out that deep mystery I see. If I could only find you." He grunted in disappointment. "If you're still alive."

The nights alone at this apartment were getting old. At least in California he stayed busy enough day and night, he rarely spent any time other than naps at his flat. The view he had in San Francisco was splendid, but not appreciated when there was no one to share it with. Tad knew when he became a detective, he would not have time for a family. Not sure if it was the slower pace here that was making him long for something more or if it was in fact the mystery in this missing woman's eyes that was making him truly want.

Sharry Hurrtz hurried home to get dinner ready for her overworked and tired man. She herself, worked a little late today. Volunteering at the community center was tiring her as well. Happy to help, though, Sharry smiled in thought, remembering the nice lady that thanked her so sweetly for helping. *It is those moments that truly make a person whole.* With dinner now in the oven, Sharry took out a new bottle of wine and poured herself a glass, sipping and smiling to herself, she imagined Len coming home and pulling off his tie. Then slowly removing his shirt and undoing his trousers, all the while staring into her longing eyes.

In a standing dream world, Sharry jumped out of her skin when the door quickly opened. "Jesus and Joseph! Lenny. You scared the devil out of me!" Lenny smiled as he recognized the look of sweet embarrassment on his wife's face.

"Got any wine for me my blushing beauty?" Sharry tried to ignore his teasing as she poured Len a glass of wine. He sipped at it slowly as he stared into the shy eyes of his wife of many years. Grinning, he said, "You were undressing me weren't you?"

Sharry snorted, and turned away. "Maybe it was some other man!"

Lenny gently grabbed her arm and turned her to him to see her lying eyes. Blushing profusely, Sharry let out another snort of disbelief.

Lenny grinned ear to ear. "Not even possible! You miss me and want me to do the stripper dance!" Laughing and pushing him away, Sharry rolled her eyes. Lenny started humming a slow tune while pulling his tie off. Sharry guffawed while blushing. Lenny took her wine out of her hand, setting it on the counter and leaned in to press a little kiss on her neck. She giggled as he started to unbutton her blouse. Their lips met, and very seductively Lenny guided his wife to the bedroom.

Agent Carson Kratz filled his coffee cup and headed to the precinct. He checked in with his borrowed crew that worked through the night on checking leads. The forensic team had left a message for him regarding the victim's cell phone. While reading his messages, Captain Hurrtz arrived. "Good morning, early bird!" Agent Kratz looked up with a nod of acknowledgment.

"My team back home said they got a little something on that short video clip."

Lenny raised his brows. "Yeah?" Carson showed him the message and they fired up Lenny's computer and waited for the enhanced video clip to pop up.

Detective Tad Billings stepped into the office. "Have we found something?" He came around the other side of the desk and all three men looked at the screen with hopeful eyes. Lenny pointed to a green car way up in the corner of the screen that was still difficult to make out, even after enhancement.

"There's our green car," Kratz noted, "It's only the front corner of the bumper but there's one of your guy's legs as well."

"Looks like he may be leaning on the car," Tad said.

"There's his shoes," Kratz added. "Get a brand and maybe we can find them."

Lenny sighed. "It's a long shot, but its more than we had before."

Cara awoke even earlier than her normal expected time of readiness for the day. Before going to her own washroom, she quietly went to Sara's room and turned the lock. Entering, she found Sara already awake staring at the dark window as if in a trance of a world she now knows has to be. "Sara, are you okay?" Cara whispered.

The woman turned to look at Cara and immediately smiled with recognition, "Cara, I missed you too! I am so happy to be here with you, finally!" Cara's face lit up like a giddy school girl. Together they both giggled and embraced in arms of love, acceptance, and promises of protection. For the first time in a very long time, Sara felt truly wanted and loved. Happy tears flowed from her weary eyes that told of little sleep.

Cara said, with excitement, "We must hurry to ready for the morning meal! We need to wear something special and be down early. I have already unpacked your bags." Cara went to the closet and opened it to a full room of scrubs in all different colors, and pretty dresses with all of the needed under garments. Sara looked amazed at all of the clothing. She barely got through the heap before Cara pulled open the dresser drawers pulling out beautiful panties and brassieres of all types and colors. Sara was in awe of how much luggage she must have had. Cara turned and opened another small door to a pullout rack of so many different shoes and boots for any weather or occasion. As they picked out clothing for her to wear for a special appearance at the morning meal, Sara was astonished how tailored the things were to her size.

"It fits perfectly!"

Cara giggled at her. "Of course it does silly! They're your clothes!" They finished dressing and hand in hand, they practically skipped down the stairs.

Miss Mam and Darci arise early to cook the morning meal. They heard the ladies coming down, so they waited with anticipation. As they entered the dining area, Miss Mam and Darci squealed their good mornings and smothered their new family member with hugs of joy. The men entered and bowed to Miss Sara throwing well-appreciated compliments as they went to their seats. Jo and Pudge slowly came in the back door to the kitchen, as they also arise before sunup to get started on the barn duties and feeding of the livestock.

After a quick clean up and changing of clothes, Jo entered the dining room first with Pudge following behind as he is always his older brother's shadow. Ever serious and overbearing, Jo's eyes went straight to Sara's. For what seemed like hours instead of seconds, their eyes connected like a force so strong, neither one could pull away. Sara knew she had to recede and show the Beast her submissiveness. For if she failed, he would surely see a challenge. That is one lesson new Sara did not forget from the old one she used to be. *Never challenge a wild animal.* Sara lowered her eyes to the floor and gave a slight curtsy and smiled a good morning as shyly as she could muster.

Jo hesitated as if deciding to himself if she truly was submissive, or if he needed to act on the stare down he received. Giving her a chance to acclimate to her new family and surroundings, he decided he would give her a day before decisions on training were needed. Or, if he decided he could no longer uphold himself to giving in to his raging desires to capture and control this irresistible female.

Miss Mam's eyes lit up as she looked to Miss Darci. "I feel we have a welcoming party to prepare for today!" Darci nodded agreement with a smile. The morning meal was cheery. Miss Mam decided to announce their plans for this evening. "We will be celebrating tonight, starting with a bountiful feast at the evening meal! Our dear newcomer will need a party! Clasping her hands together and raising her brows. "A wonderful evening of music and dance!" With smiles of agreement around the table, everyone finished their food and went to work on their chores. All must finish early in plan to prepare for the party. Jo watched as a hawk upon a mouse as Sara followed Cara to their rooms to change into scrubs. He paused outside Sara's door as he became overwhelmed with the need to try out this new version of the one who drives him to crazed sexual urges.

He felt for the key above her door, as Cara had strict instruction to always lock her in while taking care of her own needs. She is never to leave her sister on her own. Jo opened the door abruptly, purposely scaring the woman into submission. Sara jumped as she stood at the end of her bed in nothing but under garments. She instantly looked to the floor as she saw the Beast before her. He turned and re-locked the door. Sara immediately started to shake. Jo scanned the irresistible form in front of him as he moved closer. Sara tried not to shake so violently but the closer he came, the harder she trembled with well-deserved fear.

The beast grabbed her at the neck, bringing her so close to his chest, she could smell the hint of manly soap. His scent was one she had learned to fear no matter how good it may smell on anyone else. Sara fought hard the urge to back away or swing at the Beast, for if she would do so, her fate would be way worse. She forced her body to still and take whatever may follow. Jo smelled her clean hair and forced her brassiere to the floor. Sara's breasts were still bruised from the last encounter with the Beast as well as her lower extremities. She cringed as he grabbed ahold her breast and bit down on it with what felt like a wolf's tooth.

She moaned in pain, but this only encouraged him. He ripped off her panties and threw her on the bed. Sara lay, bracing for the torturous event she was getting acclimated to. He quickly stripped down to bareness. Sara noted for the first time, as he stood before her, she felt a tinge of sexual excitement. This confused her, as all she has ever felt with this man was shear pain, hatred, and the fear of evil. Jo lowered himself over his captive and for the first time since he approached this woman, he felt a slight feeling of mercy. Something in her eyes was exhibiting a softness. As he entered her with abruptness, he realized she was moist with sexual desire. He backed out of her slightly and looked down into eyes of desire. He re-entered slower and with more excitement in his erection. She groaned as he worked her along, watching her and wanting her more than ever before.

He groaned as well and bent down to take her lips onto his. They kissed like they'd hungered for so long, neither could slow the reaction. He cupped her breasts with his hands with vigor as he made wild love to her. Sara gasped as an explosion of pent-up desires released in her orgasm. Now shaking from the trauma of sexual release for the first time. Jo thrust in her with uncontrollable excitement, he ejaculated like a volcano erupting. She felt the hot lava running along the walls of her womb and down her legs. Sara's sexual yearning recharged and she reached down to caress him for more.

Jo kept the fire going until he could once more take her to orgasmic ecstasy. It did not take long for his own release once more. They lay side by side breathing heavily and processing what just happened. Sara refused to look into his eyes. Jo took her chin and pulled her face to his and kissed her vigorously. Sara dared a look into the eyes of the devil, if not only to see if the evil were still there. It was gone. Maybe only for this moment, but she would enjoy this one moment with her captor. For now she did not understand anything except the feelings she had grown. Jo caressed her gently and slid down to apologetically kiss the burns he had so easily bestowed upon her. With that, he forced himself to pull her up and carry her to the bathing room. This time he used warm water and gently washed her whole. Sara whispered a thank-you and dressed for her chores. Jo dressed as well, without a word, and took her to Cara. Her older sister looked at Sara with understanding as she kissed her on the cheek. They went to work on their chores while Jo went to the barn.

Kyra awakened alone in her bed. With a stretch and a satisfied groan, she jumped out of bed wondering when Jack left. The last thing she remembered was lying against his warm body after the most amazing night she'd ever had. Smiling to herself all the way to the kitchen, Ky opened her cupboard for some cereal. Absolutely starving, she remembered why. They skipped dinner and went straight to bed. Ky made herself pancakes, while eating bites of cereal, and started some bacon as well. The door opened as Ky went to down some coffee, spilling it down her satin wrap. "Shoot!"

Jack lazily walked in grinning, as Kyra was wiping the coffee off her now-stained satin. "Little clumsy this morning?"

"Jack Burns! There's no way I can scold you for scaring me just now." She looked straight into his deep blue eyes with a tease. "Not after the most amazing night you just gave me! Honestly, I cannot stop smiling!" She leaned towards him and very lightly touched his enticing lips with hers. "Mmm." All Jack could do was groan. He grabbed her around the waist and headed toward the bedroom groaning with need the whole way. Kyra giggled, but interrupted his plans. "The food!" He sighed and let her go turn it off, then she raced back to the bedroom, laughing and slammed the door shut.

Sharry Hurrtz woke up late. She sat up in her bed rubbing her head, as she remembered a very nice and exciting dream she had the night before. Getting up, she noted Lenny's side of the bed messed up. Confused, as Len had not slept in their bed at all since this whole missing person case started, she went to the kitchen and put water on for tea. Reaching for bread for some toast, she noticed a note on the counter. Assuming it to be a list of things Lenny needs, she dismissed it for now. Now enjoying her toast and tea, she started thinking about that dream again. Snorting it away with a gesture to herself, she finished and went to shower.

While dressing, Sharry laughed to herself as she was pretty sure last night was not a dream. Feeling so silly she went to the kitchen and picked up the note Lenny left. It read, "Good morning to my dearest love. I hope you have a spectacular day! Thank you for last night, I really needed that. I will try to leave the nuthouse of my office early so we may enjoy a nice dinner out for a change. Love and kisses, Len." Tears formed in Sharry's eyes, not from sadness, but re-found happiness. To herself, she said, "Yes, my love, today will be perfect!"

Lenny Hurrtz excused himself long enough to phone in reservations at the Breadstick Bouquet restaurant for this evening. Then he gave Sharry a quick jingle to let her know what time to be ready for dinner. He felt sorry he could not talk to her long as he had to get back to his desk that was full of conflicts to deal with. If he is going to leave a bit early, he'd better get busy.

Tad gave the captain a rundown on his plans for the case today and went back to his desk to make phone calls. Katherine's picture was staring at him again from the opened file folder on his desk. He stared at the woman the whole time he talked on the phone to possible leads on the brand of shoes in the video clip. With no luck as they just can't see enough of the shoes to identify. Tad leaned back in his chair with a sigh. Lenny peeked his head in Tad's office to let him know he is cutting out early tonight.

Tad replied, "No problem. I'll be working later tonight anyway." Then he asked, "Have you seen Burns yet?"

Lenny replied, "He's got something personal today, took the day off." Lenny shrugged his shoulders, "He's been working long hours on this case. I let him have a personal day."

Tad nodded, "No problem, no new leads to send him on anyway. If something pops up, I can handle it, or put one of the other officers on it." Lenny thanked Tad for all his dedicated hours and went back to his office.

Agent Kratz stepped in with some new information. "Hey, I got a little something." Lenny nodded him to proceed. "One of my men noticed in one of the victim's pictures you can see that the green car is gone. This is after the video clip."

Lenny in understanding, said, "That means, the car either left before she was taken, or—"

Kratz finished, "It was following behind her, which would be easier to grab her as she reached the dead zone between the residents and that convenience store."

"Exactly!"

Agent Kratz and Lenny were on the same thought process. Kratz finished with, "They may have grabbed her within sight of the store. Recheck the camera footage with a later timeline. Maybe the kid who had the phone was mistaken of where he picked it up." They hurried out of his office and grabbed Tad. Lenny filled Tad in on their hunch and all three went together to retrieve the tapes.

Jack forced himself out of the bed and pulled Ky with him. Both famished, they went to the kitchen to finish cooking the food Kyra had started. Ky sat down and put her hand to her chest with a gasp. "Work! Oh my God, I am so late! and YOU!

Aren't you supposed to be at the precinct?" Jack grinned and stole some food off her plate.

"I took the day off. Told them I needed a personal day." He mussed up Ky's hair as he told her to do the same.

Kyra looked worried as she replied, "I'm not sure I can!"

Jack threw his arms up and spit his food onto his plate. "WHAT? Of course you can. I am the police! I have to question you about the case!"

Kyra then laughed and went for her phone. The day was turning into the best shopping date she had ever had, until it all hit home. As they came out of her favorite little boutique with some lingerie fondled and picked by her flirtatious boyfriend, Ky teared up as she remembered the last time her and Kat left this boutique. Somehow knowing, Jack wiped a tear and dragged Ky to the pizza parlor for a late lunch with promises he would solve this case soon. Just for her. Pizza, beer, and a dartboard were just what she needed at the moment.

Jo spent the first part of the day butchering a pig for the evening's celebration. Excited to do so, as he had a whole different kind of feeling thumping away at his insides. A feeling he was pretty sure he had never felt before. Whistling while he prepared slabs of the pig in front of him, Pudge came into the barn and stopped, dead in his tracks. He stared at his evil brother with confusion. "Ahem." Jo looked up and smiled at Pudge. Pudge just gaped at his brother, not knowing how to approach a happy sort of Jo. "What do you need Billy?"

Still confused and borderline of a crazy kind of fear, "Um, I was just wondering if you needed me to do anything in here before we go in for the noon meal?"

Jo smiled at Pudge again. "No, I think you could take a smoke break and then I'll be ready to join you by then." Pudge just backed out of the barn as if he were escaping a haunted house. Lighting a smoke, Pudge leaned against the barn, thinking of going to town later. With Jo in a good mood, he may not notice. Jo came out and lit a cigarette. He also leaned against the barn watching the chickens pluck at the feed Pudge had thrown down. In his mind he felt like the proud rooster strutting around, keeping his hens close. He couldn't help but grin. Pudge saw him grinning again.

"What the devil got into you? Got some good weed you're not sharin' wit me?"

Jo lazily smiled towards his brother and put out his cigarette in silence. "Let's go in a little early. Save old Harry a trip."

Cara and Sara were just finishing up in the washroom off the kitchen when Jo and Pudge waltzed in. With joy written all over Jo, as he hesitated while Sara came out of the washroom. She stopped in her tracks when she saw Jo. Miss Mam glanced at the pair making such strong sexual eye contact that it gave her more cause to celebrate. She started singing loudly this time as all turned her way. She just kept on singing Joyously. Jo gave Sara a deep yearning look and her knees almost buckled. Jo realized she was weakening so he swooped her up into his arms and carried her upstairs to her room. He locked the door and all you could hear throughout the Manor was Miss Mam's joyful singing from the kitchen. It is a new and very welcomed atmosphere at the farm. Miss Mam announced to the others that Miss Sara and Master Jo would not be joining them for the noon meal, so they all ate in silence as they smiled to themselves, knowing there is a happiness in the air of a sudden. All were so very grateful and excited they would have a party to enjoy that evening.

Kratz, Hurrtz, and Billings all went over the tapes they had retrieved from the convenience store the night of the abduction. Many had already viewed them several times but only concentrating on earlier timelines. So they went forward and back and watched the clips the techs had enhanced on the computer. Lenny burst out with a shout of recognition, "That's the dumbass from the gas station the other day!"

Carson said, "It's the short guy and look at his shoes! I'll be damned!" Tad pointed out the direction the car went after stopping at the store. Lenny did the recap of order, then stared at the perp trying to bring up something in his head.

Tad asked Lenny, "Was the dumbass driving the green car?"

Lenny looked straight at Tad and said, "No! He was in an old beat-up Ford pickup. Rusty and white." Lenny hollered out for a new BOLO on the pickup truck. Tad went back to his earlier assumption. "So they were lurking on the street side and noticed the victim, then got back in their green Buick and followed her. Then jumped her, and must have put her in the trunk as no one seemed to ever see her in the car."

Tad added, "Looks like the car headed south after leaving the parking lot." Agent Kratz called out to his borrowed agents and Lenny sent out a couple of his officers to go talk to the convenience store again, and any other place of business south of that. Agents headed out to cover the south part of the county, still looking for the green car, and a rusty old white pickup, better description of the guy with the car that night.

Kratz spoke out to Lenny and Tad. "We'll find them soon, I promise." Now that we have a better description, I can order a chopper to cover the non-traversed grounds as well."

Lenny slipped out early to take his wife to a fancy night out. It had been a long time since they went out. He planned to make a night of it. Sharry was ready to go. Len changed and they went to the Breadstick Bouquet. Sharry was a bit emotional, as they hadn't been out like this in a very long time. The host took their coats to be hung and took them to a small corner table with candles lit. Sharry panicked for a tissue, as Lenny handed her his handkerchief. "I'm going to take you back home if you're going to cry all night!"

"Oh Len, I'll be fine. It's just been so long. And I really don't know why."

Lenny excused the host and helped her into her seat and sat directly across the table. Taking her hands in his, he waited for her to look at him, "I love you, Sharr, and there are two reasons we don't do this often. Number one, my job is demanding, and number two, it wouldn't be this special if we did it often." With that, he ordered a bottle of wine and an appetizer. After the waiter poured their wine, Sharry smiled and sipped her wine.

Then said, "I love you too, Len, More than you could ever imagine." The two sat in their quiet corner and exchanged small talk. Len was avoiding work as to keep this one night about just Sharr and himself. They ate and danced to a slow jazz until they were ready to go home. They laughed about everything as they went to their car. When they reached home, Len tried to carry Sharry across the threshold and failed. There they sat on the floor, half in and half out of the house, laughing hysterically. Sharry finally got herself under control and helped Lenny up. They went straight to their bedroom and shed coats and clothes onto the bed. Exhausted from the earlier hysteria, they fell asleep on top of it all.

Jack and Kyra went to the Pub and got their burger and beer. It was well past time for most people to be out, but they were still young. Sitting in a booth in the back corner where light was dim, Jack leaned in as he got Ky's attention. "I really am enjoying our time together, Ky." She smiled but held a reserved look in her eyes. Jack began again, " Moving too fast, aren't I?"

Kyra's eyes turned to apology as she replied, "Maybe a little. I don't know what it is for sure, I mean, don't take this wrong, but I think it's the case. I just feel like I cannot move on in life until I know what happened to Kat." She looked down at the table as she said, "I absolutely needed this distraction and quite frankly, a friend. I love our time together too. I just can't say this early on if it's more than the attraction."

Jack replied, "I totally understand. I'll try very hard to control my lovesick self, but I cannot possibly back down on my libido." Smiling and piercing Ky's eyes with love drunkenness, he added, "I am way too attracted to you for that!"

Kyra, all seriousness set aside, started giggling and took a long drink of her beer. "I definitely do not want you to do that!" They ate their burgers and picked at their fries, making small talk. Chatting all the way back to her apartment, about how long it took them to just go to the Pub. The rest of the night was great. Jack couldn't stay, as he needed to get back on the case the next morning. Kyra pulled herself back out of the bed. Dazzled and still naked, she smiled a well-understood thank-you once again for another wonderful day.

Jack's eyes covered the whole of her before they turned very serious as he whispered, "I think I'm in love." Kyra felt a slight panic in her gut. She kept her composure and brushed it aside as the fresh love jitters. She stared back at Jack and assured him, "It's no doubt, simply lust." He laughed and hopped up, still naked as well, Kyra couldn't help herself but stare. Ky opened the bathroom door and turned on the shower. They spent time washing each other, enjoying just the two of them. They forgot about the rest of the world for a while.

Tad and Carson teamed up to get a bite to eat. They sat at the bar and ordered food and a beer. They discussed tomorrow's plan of how they would meet for coffee and breakfast, then comb over some of the stretched-out areas. Maybe catch sight of their persons of interest. Tad thought to himself how nice it felt to just sit and enjoy a beer. He'd been working hard on the case for too long already with no break. The bar was quite full and a bit of laughter which distracted his thoughts from the case to a happy moment. Then Carson interrupted with an elbow and a smile as he pointed out a young, very good-looking woman sitting down a ways along the bar. Tad glanced her way and smiled at Carson as he nodded for him to go for it. Carson got up and moved to sit next to the lady. They sat chatting while Tad enjoyed more time away from the case.

He found his thoughts wandering to the picture of the missing young lady they'd been searching for. Emotions kept poking him as if she were family. Whispering to himself, "Why do I feel a connection to a woman I've never met? I *never* get personally involved with a case victim." Confused and frustrated, he took a large gulp of his beer and stared at the mirror on the wall behind the spirits where the woman's face instead of his own stared back at him. Every time he looked at her picture, he felt something he had never felt before. Shrugging it off, Tad ordered another beer and watched Carson as he impressed the lady at the bar with his flirtations.

Shaking his head with disbelief and thinking himself, he could never do that. He is rather proud that he does not pick up women. He is very straightforward and does not date unless he plans to keep a lady for eternity. Tad nibbled at his food and sipped his next beer as to keep his head about him. The habits of a detective never rest as Tad watched people in the mirror while he ate and drank. The door of the bar opened again with a newcomer. A short pudgy man with dirty-blond hair and a look of mischief on his rugged face waltzed in like everyone had been waiting for him to arrive.

Tad recognized the man from something or somewhere. He watched the newcomer closely as the pudgy guy waddled, as if he'd already had a few drinks, up to the bar. He ordered whiskey and scanned the room of women. Something was poking at Tad's mind as he watched this questionable character. A mind that rests on work before play, Tad took out his description of perps to watch for. Sure enough, this guy could be him. He slid off his bar stool and leisurely strolled over to Carson. He spoke low, careful to not be overheard, "What would you bet this guy to my left could be one of our men?"

Carson carefully scanned the room and did not make eye contact with the suspect. He nodded to Tad as he rose from his stool and headed out the door to check the vehicles in the lot. Meanwhile, Tad kept track of the man as he wandered over to a lone lady at a table. Carson returned with a nod to approach. Tad stood next to the table that seated a woman and the alleged suspect. "Sir, I'm Detective Tad Billings with the Lexville's Police Department."

As Carson walked up to stand next to Tad, he also identified himself. "Agent Carson Kratz with the FBI. We need you to come with us to the precinct so we can talk."

Feeling trapped, Billy (Pudge) Baur turned to the woman as he refused their suggestion.

"What's with these guys?" With a brush-off and a nervous giggle, Pudge said, "They got me mixed up with some poor guy." He shook his head and started to stand, bringing his lack of height to their wall and turned to the lady, giving a wink. "Guess I'll have to go straighten this out, little lady. Wait right here for me."

Detective Billings and Agent Kratz took Pudge by the elbows to guide him out of the establishment. Once outside, with almost a squeal, Pudge said, "Look, you guys, I ain't done a thing. I was just minding my own business." Tad pushed down on Billy's head as they pushed him into Agent Kratz's car. Carson filled the man in on the reason for taking him in for questioning as they headed to the precinct. Tad called in the captain as they arrived.

Jo was the first to start the party with pork to the table, wine, and whiskey for all. The family ate and enjoyed drinks as the waltz music played on the phonograph player. As always, Sam initiated the waltzing by approaching a lady with a bow and a hand. Such the gentleman, he loved to lavish the ladies with dance. As Sam paraded Miss Darci around the floor, Harry offered Miss Mam his humble hand. Cara and Sara were already laughing their way around the room as Jo approached. Cara gladly passed her sister to Jo with a fine lady's curtsy. By that time Sam switched from Darci to Cara and back again. Harry did the same so none of the ladies waited long.

Jo held Sara tight against him as if she would escape. She so wanted to assure him, she had nowhere to go. Her place is here with her family. She couldn't imagine leaving her sister. Her and Cara are so close. She would be devastated to lose her. Maybe she would talk to him tonight, when they are alone. The waltzing was making Sara a bit dizzy. She leaned into Jo so his body was supporting her. Jo pulled back to look down at his lady and spoke softly in her ear, "Do you need to sit down?" She answered only with a slight nod. Jo swooped her up and carried her to the chair. Instead of sitting her down alone, he sat first while holding her on his lap. He pressed his lips against her head as she leaned on him for support.

Jo waited a few minutes before pulling Sara's chin up to look into her eyes. He only saw softness and obedience. He so longed to look at this woman who makes him crazy inside, and see love there. Inside her. It seems no matter how many times he enters her, he just can't see love come forth. Jo pushed his lips to hers and demanded her return eagerness. They kissed while everyone danced and drank wine. The party went on most of the night. But it wasn't long before Jo needed to have her. He swooped her up once more, and carried her to her room for the night. There he would make love to her, until he could see love come through. Even if it took forever.

Sara fell asleep underneath her captor, the Beast. He let her sleep just long enough to be revived. Then he would wake her and love her some more. The night went on like that until morning. Jo lay staring into Sara's eyes as she woke on her own this time. She lay naked next to him, waiting for him to take her again. The Beast never sleeps is all she could think about. He started to look angry. So she reached down to caress him, hoping to keep him satisfied. He sat up, and aggressively took her face in his hands, and brought her lips to his. He kissed her almost violently, biting her lip. Sara pulled away and stared with fear. Then looked down at the bed, remembering her training. Jo got up and left in frustration. Sara was too tired to get up.

She went back to sleep until Cara came for her. She begged her sister to let her sleep, so Cara locked her door and went down to announce her sister's condition. Miss Mam approached Jo quietly to discuss his position with the Lady Sara. She bade him let her rest until the noon meal. He agreed, and went to the barn to find his brother. Pudge was nowhere to be found. Jo could hear the faint sound of a helicopter in the distance. Angry now, Jo went back to the house cursing his "pain in the ass" brother. He ordered the ladies not to answer the door if anyone came calling. Then commanded Sam and Harry to follow him to the barn. They waited outside while Jo gathered weapons and ammo for them all. The truck was gone. He knew Billy must have sneaked off last night. Jo, so angry, he wanted to kill his brother. But for now, he is on a mission. He knew he would die before he would give the girl up. She is a possession. She is his and no one else's.

The questioning began with Agent Kratz, Officer Billings and Captain Hurrtz all in the interrogation room. Billy Baur was nervously fidgeting in his chair as the men asked him his full name and address. And does he own a green car, and where is the car? What vehicle was he driving? Who is the vehicle registered to? Does he have a friend or brother who is taller than him and what color hair does he have? What is his buddy's name? The interrogation carried on as they tried to pry through the cocky disposition of the perp. The men left the room to take a break and leave Billy Baur to himself for a while. Agent Kratz grabbed a roll and some fresh coffee and sat down with the captain and detective.

"We'll let him fidget awhile, then go in with a deal to give up the other guy to get a lighter sentence. If that doesn't bring some answers, well … I do have a man undercover that can get him to talk. Under the radar, of course." Detective Billings raised his brow but turned to the captain with a nod of approval.

Captain Hurrtz replied with an approval as well and added, "We're looking at kidnapping, probably many counts and most likely murder as well." The captain stood and pushed in his chair motioning for the others to follow for lunch. Lenny Hurrtz paused at the new target area amidst all the circles and markings on the wall map of the conference room. Tad Billings stopped next to him knowing the captain would not leave the case. They are all so woven into it like silk around a worm. He, too, knows they are so close and yet so far from finding the girl.

He leaned towards Lenny's ear and said, "I'll grab you a sandwich and some coffee at the diner."

Lenny barely nodded a thank-you as he kept eyes on the map. Officers on and off duty gathered behind him as he turned hollering out, "I want all of these areas rechecked with the warrant to search the houses. WHAT ARE WE MISSING, people! It's ONE girl for Gods' sake, FIND HER!" The officers headed back out except one. Officer Wilks, a young towhead, rookie cop that was pulled out of the academy early due to the high demand for more boots on this case. Being small in build and a little leery of approaching a rather large, very ornery man, "Sir, if I could ask…."

Lenny looked at him as if he may chew him up and spit him back out. Wilks swallowed his words and stepped back but did not leave. Lenny impatiently spit at the man, "What?!"

Officer Wilks carefully approached the map pointing at an area that was not marked. "Permission to recheck this area as well? Sir?"

Lenny looked at the area he referred to. "Why?"

5

2

The officer began, "I found an old farm out there with just an old lady there." Lenny kept glaring at the man as if he didn't have all day to listen to stories. So Wilks continued, "Was just wondering myself why it's not included." Lenny stared at the map again, his mind was straining to remember what's out that way.

"Yes, and take Stoller with you."

The young officer and his partner, a heavy-set grayed man, headed out as Tad and Carson returned with the food and some fresh hot diner coffee that Len could smell as soon as the men opened the door. "Ah ... raises for you both! That smells so good." The men discussed the areas the officers were now covering for the second and some the third time. They ate and drank their coffee laughing at the thought of the perp in interrogation sweating and probably throwing up all over the floor by now.

Back at the house, Jo, Harry, and Sam all positioned their weapons at several windows and doors. They all three stayed near their designated areas of entryways. Jo gave the men of the house direct orders to shoot first and ask questions later if anyone penetrated the home. They stood watching the ladies as they kept enjoying the party until time to head to their rooms. Blowing out the lanterns and securing all entries, Jo and the men did not go to their rooms. Ma gave a nod to the men as she picked up a rifle and went to her room. Jo knew that his mother was a good shot and smiled to the men that were looking uncomfortable. They sat in chairs and quietly discussed their strategy. Just in case Billy didn't come home alone.

Billy Baur sat in the stuffy interrogation room with nothing but a cup of water while the pains in his gut wrenched. The outward exterior of his cocky disposition gave one to think he is unbreakable. His insides were churning in anxiety. Not from the police, but solely from the horrific fear of his brother. Hurrtz,

2

Billings, and Kratz all walked back into interrogation to find their subject hunched over and whining. They gasped and covered their noses as a wave of stench hit them.

Kratz exclaimed, "He shit himself, men. I would like to introduce Billy shit-ass Baur!"

Captain Hurrtz hollered out the door to the nearest officer in house, "Get him cleaned up and into a cell, and call crime scene cleanup. NOW!" The three men walked back out with a combination of disgust and laughter.

"Hey, Kratz," Billings said, "you may not need that special interrogation tactic after all!" They all three laughed over beers and burgers later that evening.

The sun was just peeking over the hillside when Harry realized he'd fallen asleep in his chair. He stretched and looked around. There was clatter in the kitchen where Miss Darci and Miss Mam were cooking up the morning meal. He stood and peeked out his window of guard and could see Sam just outside the door smoking his cigarette. He scanned the other side of the house and didn't see Jo anywhere. Then he heard heavy footsteps on the stairs. Jo was coming down. Harry gave Jo a nod of understanding and took another check out the window before sitting back down. Jo approached him saying, " Go ahead and get washed up for the meal. I'll cover your post." With another nod, Harry went to the washroom off the kitchen. Sam reentered the house, barring the front door behind him. He also gave Jo a nod and rechecked his post as well. Jo gave Sam the okay to get washed up when Harry returned. Cara and Sara came down for the meal with strict instructions they were to only help in the kitchen today near Ma and Darci. The order that Jo passed on to the other men as well, to get the women into the cellar and lock the door quickly. They all had their orders as they sat down to eat. The men were served at their posts while the women ate quietly in the dining room.

Officers Wilks and his partner Stoller, which was a heavyset man with a gruff look, napped in their car at the gas station near the southern east border of the county. Awake and fueling, they grabbed rolls and coffee and headed out to the farm he came upon previously.

The old farm was nestled in a remote area with only a two-track for a road. The only in and out of the place unless you canoed in on the river at the far back side of the property. Harry stood and raised his fisted hand and whistled. Sam and Jo both stood at attention watching as a sole police car tootled up the drive. Jo halted everyone and changed the plan. "There's only one. Let's see what they do." Jo stared at the men as a quiet instruction to hide the weapons for now. They quickly hid the rifles and put the handguns under their shirts in the back of their pants. Jo headed out the back door and Miss Mam waited at the door smoothing out her apron and hair. Sam and Harry waited off to each side of the room. The girls froze in the dining room as no one had instructed them to leave.

The officers approached the front porch with caution. The door opened as they went to knock, scaring them into attending their guns with ready hands. Miss Mam said with a nervous smile, "Hello, may I help you gentlemen?" They relaxed and introduced themselves. Officer Stoller handed her the search warrant and explained who they are still looking for. Miss Mam stepped aside and politely waved them in. She tossed a nod of assurance to Sam and Harry, and as she turned towards the dining room, she called the girls over by name.

"It's just our little family here." She turned back to the officers as they nodded to everyone. "Have any of you seen this girl?" Stoller held out the picture of Katherine Forrester. Everyone glanced at the picture except Sara. He held it closer so she could see it better. Sara gave a little clearing of her throat and carefully answered with a quiet "no." Officer Stoller gave Wilks instruction to search the upstairs while Stoller searched the main floor. When both met near the kitchen they asked about the cellar. Miss Mam gave them a nod at the door to the cellar of permission. Stoller went down the steps while Wilks stood in the doorway at the top.

Stoller only saw the room made up as a spare room and a well-stocked wine rack. He came back up and approached Miss Mam once more. "Does anyone else live here?"

Miss Mam replied, "No, sir, this is all of us." Everyone nodded in agreement. The officers thanked them all for their cooperation and left. Everyone sighed with relief and hugged their newest family member with love. They turned as Jo came in through the back door. Miss Mam gave him a welcome smile and they all went back to work except Sara. Jo picked her up into his arms and carried her upstairs, where the two of them were not seen until the evening meal.

Kyra smiled to herself thinking of how close she and Jack have become in such a short time. It is wonderful spending so much time with him. They are so good together. But a little anxiety formed deep in the pit of her stomach when reality comes back. Her best friend is still missing and she is out having the time of her life with a new boyfriend. Now crying once more, Kyra picked up her phone and made a much-dreaded call.

Jack had been working hard on Katherine's case as he knew he needed to find her for Kyra's sake. Even if it is a body recovery. He knew it was the only way Ky would further their relationship. He smiled as his phone rang and Kyra's face appeared on the screen. "Hey, beautiful!"

Kyra's heart sank at his warm greeting. "Hey. I need to talk to you tonight. Can you come by as soon as you get off work?" Jack could hear in her voice something had changed.

"Yeah, sure! We can grab dinner after that."

Kyra sighed and said a reluctant "Okay." Jack thought about nothing else the rest of the day. Kyra left work early and plopped onto her couch with a box of tissues.

Captain Hurrtz ordered the alleged perp, Billy Baur to be brought back into interrogation. Agent Kratz and Detective Billings both waited in the room. When Hurrtz and the perp came in, Agent Kratz asked Billy if he wore a diaper this time. They all laughed as Billy Baur hung his cocky attitude on the door and sat down with eyes to the floor. Kratz slammed his fist down on the table making Billy jump in his chair. "Now we have your attention" Hurrtz leaned in the corner of the room and glared at the suspect. Detective Billings pressed on with questions. Agent Kratz stood over the back of the prisoner as a hungry lioness about to pounce on its prey.

Billy kept his head down and relaxed his shoulders in submission. Billings asked for the third time, "Where do you live?"

Billy knew he could honestly say, as he could never go home now. He knew with every fiber in his being, his brother would now kill him. So, he mumbled, "I don't, I'm homeless."

Billings asked, "Where did you get the truck?"

Billy answered, " I stole it." Not getting anywhere with him, the three men left once more. Captain ordered the officer to take him away again. The three men went to the conference room, which was turned into a search and rescue base. They sat at the table discussing the reports turned in from patrolmen and women.

Lenny dropped his head into his hands pulling his hair, "It's got to be here."

Tad said, "We're missing something." Kratz grabbed the pile of papers and started over. Lenny stood up and went to the map. It was plastered with markings of where all of the residents are located. The businesses and any other buildings. Lenny put his finger on the map where his rookie officer had pointed.

"Here. Officer Wilks and Stoller went here. I remember the farm now. Used to know the family. It's been abandoned for years." Lenny turned back to the table. "Where's their report?"

Tad dug out the officers' report of the residence. "Says a family of six. All were home."

Lenny scratched his head of an imaginary itch. He grabbed the phone and called the clerk's office that would now be closing. "County Clerk's office." Lenny apologized for calling at closing.

"Can you find me anything you have on 16749 Countyline Rd? I need to know if it was purchased or sold or given or burned down etc.!"

The clerk attendant, said, "I sure will, Captain Hurrtz, but we're closing up, so it will have to wait 'til morning. "Lenny mumbled a thank-you and hung up. "First thing in the morning we need to know more about that farm." He pushed in his chair and the men all left for the day.

Sharry Hurrtz played classical music loud as she sipped wine. She and Len have been so close lately. With a renewed sex life and date out recently, she swayed herself around the kitchen, Not hearing the door. Lenny stood quietly in the kitchen entryway watching his happy wife parade around the kitchen with her wine. He didn't have the heart to be somber as he was feeling. Vowed to not bring his work home, it was in fact, still, very difficult to be as free as his soul mate. So dive in he did.

Waltzing behind her, she turned with a gasp. "Len! You scared the Be Jesus out of me!" Lenny bent his head and took his wife's lips by surprise with a long vigorous kiss.

Sharry sighed dreamily. "Are we skipping dinner?"

Lenny backed away, "NO! I'm starved, and that dinner smells more scrumptious than even you right now!"

Sharry laughed. "Now that's the husband I know." They sat at the dining room table for a change. When done, Sharry poured them a glass of wine as she told Len about her day and plans for the next. She took Len's hand in hers, and with compassionate eyes, said, "It's okay to talk about your day, Len. I've been married to a cop for many years, I can handle it." Lenny gave her a nod of relief as he squeezed her hand and filled her in on their progress with the missing girl.

Jack Burns stopped by the flower shop for a nice bouquet of assorted flowers and greens, arranged in a crystal vase on his way to Kyra's apartment. He arrived and opened the door with the flowers hiding his face. Kyra couldn't avoid a smile. Jack set the vase on the table in front of her and sat close to Kyra on the couch. He noticed her smile was a sad one. Not like he would expect from his lady when flowers are given. "What's up, beautiful?"

Ky avoided eye contact with Jack as she replied, "We need to take a break."

Jack was sure he was breathing, but it just didn't feel like it. "Is it something I haven't done or did?"

Kyra sighed, "No, Jack I'm actually very happy with you. It's just Kat. I cannot go on pretending it didn't happen so that I can go out and have fun while...." She gasped and started to cry.

Jack reached out and pulled her to him. "Just let me hold you when you need to be held, and everything else can wait." He sighed and kissed the top of her head.

Kyra stopped sobbing and whispered, "Thank you, Jack."

With that, he stood. "Do you need anything from the store?" Ky quietly shook her head back and forth while staring at the floor. Jack put his hand on her shoulder briefly, as if that may be the last time he is allowed to touch her. Sad, and a little worried Kyra may never want to see him again. And of course, in his mind, all he could think about is how she will react if they do not find her best friend alive.

He left her to her sorrows and went back to the precinct to help the other officers working the case. Thinking to himself, while eating a cold sandwich from the deli, working the case day and night, is the best thing he can do for both of them now.

Kyra ate a couple of carrots with a glass of milk and went to her bed to cry. Now, not sure if she is crying for Kat or for her and Jack. No matter the reason, it just felt good to simply cry and be alone.

The evening meal was enjoyed by all of the farm's family members. They talked and laughed and paid special attention to the newest member. Sara had never been a part of, what most people would call a normal family. She only remembered her mother. It had always been that way. Her mother never told her about any family. Sara spoke out at the meal for the first time since arriving at the farm. With only the short memory of her arrival to be with her sister Cara and the others, Sara was so very thankful for all they have done for her. So she stood and said so with a shy smile. It seemed everyone talked at once, while Miss Mam came around the table to hug her newest daughter. Happy tears filled everyone's eyes as they all in turn followed Miss Mam's approach.

They all took wine except for Jo, Sam, and Harry. The three men sipped coffee as they knew they would still be on watch. Jo called the men over to the front window for a huddle away from the ladies. Looking at Sam and Harry with complete seriousness, "We'll take turns on watch starting tonight. We will do so until Billy returns. As long as he is not here, we have to assume the police could return anytime." Harry and Sam nodded a firm agreement.

Sam said with dutiful chin high, "I can take the first shift, sir."

Harry mumbled low, looking at Jo, "I'll take second." Joe nodded in agreement. "That's perfect. I'll rest up and relieve

Harry at midnight." With that, Jo let Ma know the plan. Miss Mam motioned for the ladies of the house to follow her to the kitchen. They all brought their wine and cleaned up from evening meal while Miss Mam reminded them of the plan. Just in case they should get more visitors. Miss Mam did not sing openly this night. Instead, she lay ready in her mind of what she will need to do, should anyone try to take her family. Jo came to the kitchen before going up to what he now claims as his room. Which is anywhere his quarry lies, is where he lies as well. He pulled Sara aside with a motion to follow. Sara immediately hung close to her captor as she obediently stayed behind him, up the stairs, to the room that she now shares with the master. As he opened the door to their room, Jo stood to the side, waiting while his, and only his, woman went in. Sara kept her eyes to the floor and presumed to undress as the beast closed the door.

Downstairs, Sam perched himself for the evening. He watched the night like a hawk not willing to share his prey. Harry, not wanting to be far from his post, laid on the settee in the front parlor for a nap. Doris and Cara went up to Cara's room. They bunked together in case they needed to go to the cellar in a hurry. Whispering to each other their worries of the family. Miss Mam lay awake holding her shot gun across her arms. Talking as if someone were standing before her, she said, "That girl is our property. She must be protected at any cost." Miss Mam could not stop smiling in a giddy way. She thought how much jo has changed since that cute little girl came here. She's never seen him so determined and happy. In his sort of way of course.

Jo dozed off with Sara lying beside him. Eyes open, staring at the darkness as if a monster were waiting for her eyes to close. Jo stirred next to her and she startled. He turned toward her and instantly jumped up with rifle in hand. He snorted like the devil himself, sporting fire in his eyes as he looked around the room.

Sara lay shivering and barely whispered, "You scared me." He turned to her from across the room with confusion on his brow. Again, almost a whisper, "It was you."

Setting down his weapon, he grumbled annoyance back to the bed. He pulled the covers from her and took her one more brutal time before leaving to man his post. Sara still lay quiet. Shivering with fear of a monster outside their world, that may come and rip her away from her family.

Jo appeared as Harry stood with a nod. He questioned, "Still no Billy?" Harry gave a regretful no. Sam had fallen asleep on the settee this time, so Harry went to his room with rifle in arms. Jo sat quietly, thinking of the woman he left in the bed. His heart began to race at the thought of losing her. Anger filled his nostrils 'til he thought he would explode. He stood as a soldier and paced back and forth until light from the morning rise shone in through the window. He went out onto the porch to smoke and listened to the early morning rituals of nature. The rooster was crowing near the barn and the hens were scurrying about, pecking at the ground. The birds at the top of the trees sat silent as if they could sense turmoil in the air so chilling they just couldn't chirp. A deep dread, not from the cold, ran through Jo's bloodstream as he knew a war was coming.

Captain Hurrtz went straight to the coffee station after arriving to work with determination on his mind. Then with a full cup, he checked in with the night crew and added more notes to the case board on the wall. He looked at that area of the old farm as he keyed the county clerk's office number into his phone. On the other end a woman's voice addressed the call firmly stating the hours of operation. Hurrtz grumbled and hung up the phone. He turned to Detective Billings as he came through the door. "We got anything more on that old farm yet?" Tad clapped his hands together and started looking through papers and messages left. Tad looked at the captain with compassion for the stress the man was feeling.

"Tell you what, I'll go down to the clerk's office in person and get that info for you! As soon as they open." Lenny raised his brow and thanked the man with zeal. Tad went through the coffee drive up and then sat outside the clerk's office with patience and Katherine Forrester's picture. Looking into the eyes of the missing girl was like looking into neverland. Intrigue, compassion, and mystery all there. To himself, he asked, "But is she real? And where? I feel as though I'm chasing a fairy tale." A lady unlocking the door of the clerk's office back entrance, broke Tad's thoughts. He hopped out of his car and followed the County Clerk to her desk. "I'm Tad Billings from the precinct," he explained, flipping out his badge. "I need any and all information you have on the old farm on Countyline Rd."

The lady smiled. "Yes, your captain called yesterday at closing." She then took her notes to the public counter and motioned him over. "Address, 16749?" Tad nodded and waited as the woman went to the files and pulled out a rather thick folder. She laid it in front of Tad and motioned him away. Tad hesitated in confusion. Holding the folder out toward her, "Don't you need to make copies and keep the folder here?"

The woman smiled again and replied, "I did that last night." Tad gave her a look of disbelief. The woman simply shrugged her shoulders and tilted her head. "I owed him." Tad smiled knowingly and turned for the door. The woman hollered to him as he opened the door, "Tell Len we're even." Tad nodded and left.

Sara dressed and waited near the window for Cara to come for her. Knowing the days are long of late as they all mind their chores, but in the pit of their stomachs, they all know what lies ahead. Sara took a deep breath to ease the nervous jitters as the door to her room opened. Cara stood with a quiet stern on her expression. Sara dipped into a teasing curtsy, making light the dreaded future. Cara giggled and grabbed her silly sister's arm as they went down the steps to help get the morning meal onto the table.

Miss Mam was her cheery, confident self, as she laid out the meal, and threw commands out for all the meal necessities. Darci brought out the usual dishes, looking to the others to place settings onto the table. All of the men filled their plates and went to their posts of guard for the day. Miss Mam noticed Jo still at his post, so she handed Sara a bountiful plate of eggs, potatoes, and greens. She nodded toward Jo and Sara took the plate to the master. He looked at the plate and grumbled. Sara waited for instruction. Jo pointed to a small table next to him and Sara obeyed and returned to the dining room. Everyone picked at their food as if lacking appetite. There were many scraps fed to the pigs that morning.

Tad went straight to Lenny's office with the file folder he carried tightly guarded under arm. Lenny looked up and then to the file. "Well?"

Tad pulled up a chair opposite Lenny. "I haven't had time to thoroughly read everything, But seems obvious with the most recent occupants being the original owners, that have passed on years ago, we surely have squatters." Lenny took the folder from Tad and verified what he was told.

"Looks that way." He questioned Tad as he looked up from the folder. "Are we sure it's not family of the deceased?"

Tad took his notes from his own folder he held. "I've checked every surviving family member on that tree." Lenny stood with determination as he motioned Tad to follow. With Tad at his heals the, two filled in Carson with the new lead as they all went to the case wall. Captain Hurrtz hollered orders to the crew of officers working on the case. They all gathered around the table and Hurrtz explained the current situation. Detective Billings and Agent Kratz handed out the address of said farm. They were all instructed a plan of a second search of the farmhouse and identifying the current dwellers in question. Kratz called in a request for warrants to extend their search to all buildings and property at said address. Jack Burns made sure he was included in this raid on the farm. He wanted to be the one to give Kyra firsthand information on the results.

Jo paced impatiently as his gut wrenched with the knowledge of what was to come. Still no word from his brother. He knew deep in the pit of his gut the stupid ass had gotten himself arrested. For drunk and disorderly no doubt. But Jo couldn't let his guard down until he knew for a fact it is only about him and his behavior. If they have a description of him grabbing the girl off the street, he would bring hell down on them all. Sam mumbled to himself a prayer for protection from the good Lord himself as he watched Jo pace nervously. Harry was the only one calm, and at the moment, on the front porch dragging long hard puffs from the tobacco stick between his lips. The women quietly tended their chores and the only sound was footsteps on the hardwood floors.

Jo deadened his steps immediately when his hawklike vision narrowed in on the front of a police cruiser slowly crawling toward the farm between the trees. He acted quick with yelled commands to the other watchmen. That was the cue for the ladies as they ran to the cellar locking the padlock on their side of the door. Jo looked to each man a stern glare that demanded fight at any cost.

The first car approached slowly as a second car held back. Jo retracted himself from the post and quietly sneaked out the back door, while Sam took charge of the door. Harry held back out of sight. Officer Stoller waltzed up the front steps and knocked on the door with a warrant to arrest all on the property for squatting on private property. Sam cracked the door ajar.

Officer Stoller offered his warrant, "I have this warrant to arrest all present until we get the legalities worked out of this property." Sam turned a look of question to Harry. He came forward and explained that they were here as guests, and the officers would need to come back when the owner was present. Sam repeated Harry's firm statement. Officer Stoller pulled out his handcuffs and answered, "That may be, but you folks will still need to come to the station with me to work this out. You can come willingly or make it hard." Sam carefully looked from right to left of the property, realizing they were surrounding the farm. He turned to Harry with a mutual understanding of plan B. Harry nodded and they both put the rifles down and opened the door.

In the cellar the ladies whispered to each other a plan to elude the search. Miss Mam uncovered a trapdoor in the cellar identical to the one in the barn. She hurried the girls down and closed the door quietly behind them, recovering the trapdoor.

As the officers entered the farmhouse, Sam and Harry assured them there was no one else home. Detective Billings, Agent Kratz, and Captain Hurrtz all entered to help with the search. Officer Stoller motioned them to the cellar door that he had previously searched. Agent Kratz demanded the door to be unlocked. No one budged. Miss Mam stayed quiet holding her rifle aimed at the door. Captain Hurrtz then hollered for an officer to shoot the door handle until it opened. And so the shots rang out 'til the door swung open and return fire hit Agent Kratz and the officer.

The captain yelled, "Officers down!" Everyone backed away as Miss Mam kept firing. She shot and reloaded as fast as a western gunslinger. Hurrtz ordered a full-out open fire until they breached the steps and gained control of the room. Miss Mam was hit several times before falling to the floor, dropping her rifle and the handgun that was kept in the cellar. Her pulse was checked and announced deceased. Captain Hurrtz ordered the remaining officers to search and seize the rest of the property.

Jo stayed back as he knew he would not win against so many. His gut wrenched with anxiety as he lay watching who was brought out of the house. He saw Harry and Sam taken but no sign of the ladies. Determined they were not taking the only thing in this world worth living for.

Not long after the showdown with, he assumed, was his Ma, ambulances came. He watched from hiding as two bodies were taken out on gurneys Jo lay low on the ground behind foliage into the woods waiting for the ultimate fight.

What seemed like days was only hours before the cars started leaving with only a few detectives and officers doing leg work. They took pictures before sealing off and locking the premises down. A bloodied sheet covering the head of a victim on a gurney was finally taken away. That Jo presumed was his mother. He looked away. But only brief shame and regret was felt as he brushed the feelings away as if a comrade soldier had fallen. The only maternal feelings he had for his mother were drowned out early in childhood. Over the years, Ma had become a partner in business. He waited still. No sign of the other three women.

Agent Kratz lay in the hospital with wounds to the arm and shoulder. He was caught by some of the shotgun spray that hit the officer next to him. He, however, did not make it. Most of the shots hit him dead on, giving him fatal shots to the chest and gut. Hurrtz and Billings put officers to work on the paperwork of the day's showdown and posted guards from the FBI outside Kratz's hospital room. There were guards placed at the farm as well. Officer Wilks and Stoller stated there to be three women residents missing.

Captain Hurrtz and Detective Billings sat in the conference room with Officer Burns and Stoller and Wilks. "Where the devil is the partner and the other missing women?"

Hurrtz slammed his fist down on the table in frustration. Billings shook his head and Burns offered, "Maybe the partner got away with the women?"

Billings looked over the list of seized items. "Says five rooms occupied in the upstairs. Two downstairs, and a spare room set up in cellar."

Burns spoke up. "We have two men that claim everyone is accounted for. I'm guessing they're protecting someone."

Billings added, "And what about the barn setup? I mean, you have to know how to butcher and process meat to have such an expensive set up."

Hurrtz chimed in, "Someone with brains and know how, which is not the half we have in custody."

Wilks added, "Maybe the old man Harry?" One of the men spoke, "He said he only takes care of the grounds." Hurrtz said, "And Sam says he does the maintenance. So that only leaves the missing partner or the perp we have in custody." Stoller put in, "Maybe the old bitch that killed our officer was the butcher." They nodded with shrewd comments. Hurrtz announced, "Let's try to get a good night's sleep." With a long sigh, he added, "Cause we are all required to attend and assist the FBI at the break of dawn, with a search party." The men all grumbled as they stood.

Stoller sighed. "Yeah, how can we get so lucky?"

Billings smiled. "Just load yourself up on caffeine and steroids, and you'll blend in!" Hurrtz gave a chuckle as they all left to find peace for a few hours. That was all they had left before the crack of dawn, FBI bugle blow.

Cara, Darci, and Sara whispered back and forth. They planned to stay in the shelter as long as they had water and food. Both underground shelters at the farm were stocked with everything needed to survive for at least a month. They couldn't hear anything, but assumed the worst until the master comes to get them.

The night lay quiet and the guards watching the old

farmhouse took regular breaks. Two in back and two in front was all Jo noted. He used stealth and training from his war history to quickly and quietly sneak up on the unsuspecting officers. He took the first one out with his hunting knife and held the other with threat at the end of his gun. He went in the back door with the officer in front of him for cover. No one was inside. He gagged and bound the man and hid him in the washroom off the kitchen. Then quietly went to the front and distracted the guards with a noise inside the door. The officers turned with a jolt of surprise. One stayed outside with weapon drawn toward the house and the other man approached the porch. As he opened the front door he hollered out for the guards in back. No one answered so he motioned the officer behind him to go around back. He slowly entered and was greeted by a blow from behind.

The other officer found the dead colleague on the ground. He radioed for backup. His partner that entered in the front of the house wasn't answering. He waited among the bushes behind the house.

Hurrtz, Billings, and Burns all heard the call. With emergency pumping through their veins, they raced to the farm. Sirens blaring down the two-track and dust filling the air, cops came from all directions as they used their cruisers to surround the house. The officer waiting jumped from the bushes and filled them in on the circumstances. Three officers presumed down. More ambulances were on the way. The perp was inside the house and one officer is verified dead.

Captain Hurrtz got there behind the ambulances. He jumped from the car yelling, "Dammit! Get this guy! He's killed two of our own, possibly more." The new officers on the scene went into the house with weapons blazing. They were determined. They were not walking away without this perp dead at their feet. The house was full of cops. Off duty and on duty. They found another officer just coming around as he lay helpless on the floor.

Still looking for the fourth guard, they combed every inch of that place. Finally, Burns hollered out, "Found him!" They all ran over in excitement for the kill.

Burns put his protective arm out with eyebrows raised, "Down men! He's ours!" They all backed down and returned to the hunt. Burns pulled the gag off the officer and untied his hands. Sighing with apologies to his fellow officer, he held out his hand to help him up. The officer thanked him and went on his own hunt and peck.

He whispered to Burns, "I heard the son of a bitch open the cellar door, and he never came back up the stairs." Burns grabbed two of the officers from the hunt and all four of them headed down the cellar stairs. Burns in the lead, motioned to the men behind him in silence to go to each side of the cellar. quietly they searched and came up empty. The officer from the original guard post whispered to Burns, "Gotta be here somewhere." They heard a slight noise and all looked down. Part of the space rug was turned up. Burns bent down and carefully pulled back the rug and saw the trapdoor.

He motioned quietly for one of the men to get him a smoke bomb from the task van. They all waited in silence until the man returned. In a carefully quiet manner, one man started to lift the cover as another quickly threw in the bomb. Shots rang out at the entry area. All four men stayed back until finally three women crawled out coughing and gagging. Men from upstairs came barreling down the steps from the sound of shots fired. In the front of the stampede was Billings and Hurrtz. The officers waiting at the entry to the shelter had guns drawn and ready.

Hurrtz went over and yelled, "It's over man, Come on out. We know you're in there. Save us all grief and a couple more lives including your own by giving yourself up." Behind them, the ladies were being helped up the stairs and escorted to the ambulance to be looked at. Billings took charge of the questioning of the ladies. He started asking them why they hid, when more gunshots were heard from the house. Everyone jumped and turned towards the house. The three ladies looked horrified. Billings turned back to the ladies and caught eye contact with one of the three. Their eyes locked as Billings stared into the same world that had been haunting him since this case began.

He smiled and reached out to the woman. "I didn't catch your name." The woman looked scared and kept silent. Another of the women turned to him and answered, "I am Cara, that's Darci, and this is my sister Sara."

Detective Billings introduced himself and looked confused. He asked again as the shorter woman, Sara, turned away in avoidance. Cara protectively put her arm out to guard her sister. Detective Billings pulled out the picture of Katherine Forrester. He held it up as the lady turned away once more. He couldn't be positive, but damn sure he was looking at the same face and eyes. If he could get her to smile, he would know for sure. He left the ladies with two armed men and took the paramedic aside. "Get blood from these ladies immediately and send it to the lab marked urgent."

The paramedic responded, "Consider it done." He turned back to the officers guarding the ladies and ordered, "Do not let them out of your sight, or I'll make sure your badges are suspended." With that, he went to the house as they were bringing out a body. He stopped the gurney's path and pulled the sheet back. As he did, a cry of terror rang out from one of the ladies. The woman in question fell to her knees in devastation as the officer held her back.

"NOOOOO!" She, Sara, cried in horror as she saw who was under the bloodied sheet. Cara hugged her sister in comfort, crying herself. Not for the master, but for her sister's broken heart. Sara dropped her head to the ground wailing. Tad Billings watched the scene play out with extreme sadness and compassion for who he knows now, as the abducted woman who has haunted them all for so long.

As the gurney was put into the ambulance, Billings hollered, "Wait!" Understanding the situation, he went to the ladies and helped the woman in question, Sara to her feet and brought her to the ambulance to say goodbye. For closure. He knew in cases like these, cases he had been involved with, the victim needed to see the villain gone before healing could begin. With pained and grief-stricken orbs, Sara thanked him softly in whimpers as she laid her hand upon the lifeless body before her.

Then laying her head against him she cried. Everyone around her hung their heads in understanding and respect. Cara hugged her tight as she pulled her from him. She whispered comforting promises that she still has her and will always be here, with her. Sara turned and squeezed her sister so tight Cara could hardly breathe. Tears rolled down their cheeks as they were guided back to the other ambulance. Once again, three ambulances pulled away from the farmhouse.

Lenny Hurrtz and Tad Billings followed the ambulances to the hospital with guards assigned to all.

Officer Jack Burns went straight to Kyra's apartment and let himself in. Kyra stood staring, holding her breath, in wait of dreaded news she wasn't sure she wanted to hear. Jack sighed a relief as he told her what happened. Kyra covered her face as tears filled her hands. "Oh my God! She's okay?!" Jack embraced Ky as she wept with relief and happiness. "When can I see her? Oh my God, thank you! Thank you, God! You have to take me to her, Jack!"

He held Ky back and pulled her to sit on the couch. "You can't see her yet. She's a little … well, she doesn't seem to re-member or refuses to say who she is. Kyra looked puzzled. Jack continued, "She will need a lot of therapy and she is currently incarcerated."

Ky exploded, "INCARCERATED? Why? She's a victim,

Jack! Why the hell would she be arrested?"

Jack tried to calm her down to explain the situation better. "There are so many questions right now. They are trying to get answers and straighten the mess out. I'll stay here tonight and take you first thing in the morning to see her."

Kyra sighed, "Thank you." She went to the fridge and grabbed two beers. Jack reached out with a heavy thanks for the beer he desperately needed. Ky pulled it away, "Hell no, these are both for me!! You're on your own!" With mouth open from shock and disappointment, Jack got up and got his own beer. Kyra guzzled the first one down, as Jack watched in amazement.

"Just when I think I know you." Kyra laughed and they hit their beers together in cheers.

Lenny and Tad checked in on Agent Carson Kratz. They brought him out of a well-needed sleep. "Hey, how's our vest doing?"

Carson, still groggy, gave a chuckle as he turned in his bed to face them. "Next time you're going first!"

Lenny laughed, "Don't bet on it!"

Tad went to the opposite side of the hospital bed and shook Kratz's hand on his good arm. "How's it going in here, man?"

"You know, keeping the nurses entertained!"

Tad replied, "Even the male nurses?" They all laughed and discussed everything except the case.

The doctor came in and broke up the party. "All right, men, he needs his rest." Lenny signed off and went home. He knew Sharry would be waiting with food and wine for him. Tad on the other hand, stuck around. He went down to the room with the ladies that are spending the night under observation. He tapped on the door after checking in with their guard outside the door. Cara carefully opened the door. Relieved to see it was him. The man that actually cared about them and was very kind. She smiled in a kind gesture.

"Come in." Tad reminded them of his name and position in the precinct. They nodded in understanding. Sara was more leery of him than Cara or Darci.

Sara asked softly, almost in fear, "Are we in trouble for hiding?" Her eyes were yearning and telling him a story of fear yet submissiveness. This, he knew from experience, was a very delicate situation. He knew he had to be careful how he delivered his questions. And to never speak of her captor as a villain. "No, I think we understand why you would hide. It had to be extremely frightening to have the police raid the farm." Sara looked down as if she was afraid to admit the fear that had branded her for the entirety of her experience at the farm. But also he understood her loyalty to her captor. That, too, had been branded into her whole being, undoubtedly with force. He questioned Cara first, to instill some trust in Sara's presence, before he turned to her. Cara gave him some answers.

Now he wanted to hear Sara's story. "How did you come to live at the farm?" Sara looked to Cara first. This told him she is saying what she was told to say. But that is okay. He knows if he gets her comfortable with talking to him, she will eventually tell him the real story.

"I wanted to be with my sister, Cara. So, I came to the farm to be part of the family." Tad accepted her answer, even though he knew it was a lie. He stood with a sigh of tiredness, "Okay, ladies, I just wanted to check on you before I went home. You need to rest tonight. I'm going to get some sleep too. It's been a long day for all of us." He smiled with compassion at them as he left, closing the door behind him. He let the officer have a break. Sitting outside their door, made him feel protective. After the long search behind them, the last thing he wanted was to lose her. The shorter, womanly curves, seductive eyes. Tad let out a smitten sigh as he asked the nurses to bring him a cot to sleep on. Detective Tad Billings never left the hospital.

Morning came too quick for Jack Burns. Kyra jumped out of bed so fast, Jack thought there was a fire. Ky laughed for a minute, then she ordered him up. "Come on Jack, we need to go. I want to see Kat." Jack grumbled through his shower that she let last two minutes. Then she nearly shoved a doughnut in his mouth and handed him a to-go cup of coffee. Then they were on their way to the hospital. Jack reminded Ky of her friend's condition and to not expect much from her. Kyra nodded in acceptance. They approached the nurses' station. Ky saw the officer outside the door. She gave him a look of disgust to his keeping her dearest friend prisoner.

Jack shrugged his shoulders to the officer with a silent lipped apology. He nodded complete understanding to Jack. He stepped in front of the door to guard it as Kyra tried to grab the doorknob. She stared in challenge at the officer. Jack pulled her away from the door and motioned her to sit on the chair and wait for permission. Kyra sat with a long-exaggerated sigh. The doctor came from the room and Detective Billings. Kyra jumped up to confront the doctor on Katherine's condition. Dr. Helser asked if she was family.

Kyra said, "Practically!" The doctor turned to the detective for assurance. "If you don't have any objection?" Detective Billings took Jack and Kyra to a waiting room down the hall.

"I'm sorry to ask you to wait for visits. Katherine is still under watch and being evaluated." Tad sighed as he looked at Jack for assistance in getting through to Kyra.

Jack sat Kyra down and re-explained Kat's condition. "We don't know if she will even recognize you right now."

Kyra looked at the detective with determination. "Why don't we just try? Maybe seeing me will help bring her back to this life."

Billings hesitated. "It could also put her in a deeper state of denial."

Jack offered, "How bout we try walking in, and acting like

nothing happened, and see how she reacts to Kyra."

Tad gave in, even though it was against his professional judgment. Kyra took a deep breath as she opened the door and slowly stepped in. She tried not to react when she saw Kat's hair cut off and a deep red that surely matched the gal next to her. It was like the world just stopped suddenly, to see her best friend sitting there. She looked and seemed like a whole different person to Kyra. She had to stop herself from turning around and running, never stopping. She tried to smile and say something. She just froze. Tears welled up in her eyes, and she simply couldn't speak. Cara stood and introduced herself and then introduced her sister Sara and Miss Darci. Ky didn't know what to say.

Jack stepped in front of Kyra to divert attention away. He apologized to the ladies and turned Kyra around guiding her toward the door. Then they heard a soft voice, almost a whisper, "I think I know you. Don't leave."

Kyra started to cry and turned back around to face Kat. Sara started to cry also. Ky reached out for Kat, moving closer to the bed where Kat was sitting, until she could wrap her arms around her. They hugged tight, while both cried.

Captain Hurrtz got coffee on his way to the hospital. What a week. Injured and dead officers. Perps dead and many witnesses to interview. Talking to himself is what kept him sane. He relieved the officer guarding the door of the lady witnesses. Upon entering the room, the captain found the ladies chatting quietly. "Good morning, ladies. I hope you rested some. It was quite an event yesterday." They all stood as if they were addressing the man in charge. "Ladies, I know you haven't been separated since you got here." He cleared his throat. "I will be taking all of you to separate rooms. Do you understand?" They nodded in unison.

The captain knew there was no way the missing woman

would speak out if they continued to keep them together. He left the taller woman, Cara there and took the other two. He saw no reason they shouldn't start the questioning here, before their release from the hospital to the precinct. He started with the missing woman, Katherine/Sara. Detective Billings found them via the nurses' station when he returned from the cafeteria. He joined the captain, but stood in the shadows to see the woman's behavior to the questioning without the other women in the room.

He sipped his coffee as he watched her. If it weren't for those telltale eyes, one would never see the missing woman there in front of them. Captain Hurrtz started with simple questions of her past. The line of questions needed to tell them what all and for how far back she remembers. This will enlighten them on the level of PTSD she has suffered. It will also give them an idea of who to assign to her therapy from here on out. Sara/ Kat, answered all the questions of past memories with the same sincere answer of simply, "I don't remember."

The captain moved to more recent events. "Do you know how you got to the farm?"

She thought hard and looked to the window, then at Detective Billings and replied, "NO."

The captain did not push for anything beyond the simple structure of his goal. He took out pictures from the crime scene one at a time asking her to identify each person if she could. Sara/ Kat looked at the first picture he held out. She responded quickly, meaning she knows the people she was with quite well. The first one was Miss Mam. She could not however say her real name. Only as the woman in charge. Next was the black man, resident. "That is Sam." The captain thanked her each time she helped with a name. It was a show of appreciation and a will to try hard to help. She went on to identify the rest of the family members who shared the farm, with The Master/Beast for last.

His picture brought deep hurt and emotion as his picture

was of him dead. She hesitated with tears rolling down her cheeks. The captain cooed her to take her time, there is no need to rush. They in fact knew exactly who he was. They needed to hear her identify him. How she perceived him said a lot about her level of position with him. With difficulty, Sara/ Kat, spoke with the kind of emotion that could only come from either complete brainwashing or true love.

Deciphering which would be up to the psychologist in therapy. Only then would they be able to decide in a court of law that she is or is not liable for the pending charges of the squatting and activities that took place in the barn. Was she there of her own free will with knowledge of the crimes being committed or was she in fact abducted and forcefully brainwashed to a point of losing her real identity.

The same went for all of the residents involved. They questioned them all in the same manner to determine their knowledge of crimes. All were being incarcerated until decisions were made in court of their future.

Back at the precinct Hurrtz, Billings and the FBI agents discussed the case in detail. They went over the possible barn activities. Some of the initial answers given gave them more questions. Hurrtz asked, "Billings, what's your take on some of this?" He took a gulp of his coffee and pointed to the equipment they seized from the barn. "What I want to know is, what the devil was that used for?" The pictures spread out on the table were of typical butcher operations except one. Billings picked up the picture to make sure all present were seeing the same thing he was seeing.

One of the agents squinted as he moved closer to the picture to make no mistake, "Is that…? What? It's a guillotine!" Tad Billings laid the picture back down and raised his eyebrows in question. "That is the defining part of this equation I am the most curious about." The other agents and Hurrtz all agreed the line of questioning needed to focus on that piece of equipment's part in all of this.

Billings added, "And what happened to the other missing homeless people?" All agreed with expressions of serious disturbance. With that, Captain Hurrtz called out for a new batch of officers, with Stoller in charge, to go back to the farm ASAP, and check the grounds deeper for evidence of the other missing people.

Billings went back to the hospital to check on Agent Carson Kratz and to see if their other farm residents were ready for release yet.

Agent Kratz was up and packing when Billings came in. "Leaving already, Vest?"

Kratz turned with a chuckle, "Hell yes! We have a case to tally up!"

Billings replied, "That we do. I'm glad you're up for the challenge, because the whole thing just took a turn for the rare and unusual."

Kratz looked on with curiosity. "Yeah?"

Billings smiled broadly. They headed to the nurses' station outside their ladies' three rooms. "They ready for transport yet?"

The head nurse on duty answered with a smile, "They're all yours."

"All right," Billings said, "I'll get officers here to get them out of your hair!" She nodded with relief. He made the call to the precinct to send over a wagon for their transport. Another quick call to the captain to be expecting his prisoners.

Hurrtz turned to the agents. "Last three on their way over. That gives us six alleged questionable perps to pick and poke at!" The agents all nodded readiness.

Kyra went to Kat's townhouse to freshen it up with confidence that she would be cleared to go home soon. She texted Jack's personal number and left a message that she would be at Kat's. Then she got busy wiping down the kitchen with fresh citrus scents and the bathroom she cleaned with lavender. Kyra hummed while vacuuming and dusting the spacious apartment. This is what Kyra has been waiting for. Kat to come home. It's like a dream. Everything back to normal. She sighed a happy exhale as she finished the chores.

Jack read the message from Ky and felt a ping of anxiety. He couldn't help but worry how this new situation would affect their relationship. As he stared at his phone with a scrunched-up face, Tad Billings joined him with his own anxieties.

"Is it serious?"

Jack looked up suddenly as if startled. "Ah … you have no idea!"

Tad responded, "Probably do." Jack just shook his head back and forth. Tad offered, "We could skip out early and grab a beer and a bite and talk about it."

Jack replied, "That sounds good." With that, Jack texted Kyra he would not be over tonight. He needed to get a beer with his buddy and go over some stuff.

Ky got his message and went back to her place alone. Being alone for a night would probably do her some good. *Besides,* she thought to herself, *we're supposed to be taking a break.* She grabbed her own beer from the fridge and curled up with a book to take her mind off everything for a while.

Tad checked in on Sara/ Kat. She looked very tired and stressed. He felt so much compassion for this woman. There she was, on her way to a Halloween party and WHAM, all of a sudden her whole world is upside down. She was being held in a jail cell. Tad put his hands on his hips and let out a snort of disagreement. He found the captain and with an aggravated tone, said, "We need to get Katherine somewhere comfortable with around the clock care."

Hurrtz asked, "Why?"

"Have you seen her today?"

"Not yet." Billings took the captain's arm and pulled him along. They stood in front of Katherine Forrester's cell where she lay on the cot staring at the wall as if there were no world left around her. The captain took one look at her and agreed. They made arrangements for her to be moved to a rehabilitation center with twenty-four-hour care. There she would also receive psychological therapy. Tad Billings sat with Katherine until they came to transport her. He tried to make conversation, but she did not reply. She had clearly sunk into a state of shock. It was nearly an hour before an officer came to get Katherine. Tad was relieved to have it be a woman with a lady therapist to ride along and get her settled into a room. Tad personally thanked the captain before cutting out for the day with plans of a beer with a buddy and a long visit with the Lady Katherine in the morning to make sure she was getting the care she needed.

Sharry Hurrtz received a call from her husband that set her into motion as a personal caregiver and friend for Katherine Forrester. Sharry was briefed by the nurse at the facility of her needs to just have the same reliable person there for her the same time every day. Sharry used to be a nurse a long time ago. She had given up her career to do volunteer work where needed and to enjoy being a housewife for Lenny. With his stressful and personal consuming job, it just felt right.

Katherine was only in her new room at the rehabilitation center about an hour or so when Sharry Hurrtz came in as a support caregiver. She introduced herself and she did some personal grooming with the young woman. She knew that just little things like brushing her hair and talking to her in an even light tone would be therapeutic.

She showed her how to operate the TV remote for when she was alone in the evenings, and set up her bathroom personals. Sharry noted, still no response from the woman.

But she stayed the rest of the day and talked with the nurse and therapist. Then went home to get dinner going for Len.

Tad met Jack at the pub. They ordered a pitcher of beer from the tap and burgers. Tad gave Jack the address and room number for Katherine Forrester's new location to pass on to Kyra. "Thank you ... that's actually what's eating at me." Tad took a gulp of his beer and motioned with his hand to continue. "Before Kat was rescued, Kyra asked for a break in our relationship until Kat was found."

"Seems reasonable."

Jack shrugged agreement. "But now ... well, it seems she's expecting everything to go back to normal with Kat." He paused and sighed with frustration. "She doesn't quite get it. That her best friend is very messed up."

Tad nodded agreement and replied, "That is an understatement. This woman is going to take a long time to heal and will probably always have some PTSD to deal with."

"How do I get through to Ky without causing *us* more problems?"

Tad took a bite of his burger and another drink and thought hard before answering. "I would say, be the one who takes her to visit the woman every day until Kyra is comfortable going alone. And make sure she talks with the therapist for ways to work with Katherine in a healthy way."

Jack raised his brows. "Wow, you talk like you know all about this stuff!"

Tad did a long sigh before offering a cheers with his beer. They finished their beer and made small talk until it was late. Jack took off and Tad stayed longer drowning the past with more beer. A woman joined him smiling as if they had been lovers. Tad always avoided flirting. He stared at her in question. "Can I help you with something?" The woman offered to stay for a while and see what happens. Tad grabbed his tab and went to the bar to pay. He never looked back and said nothing to the strange woman before leaving. He heard her holler "ASSHOLE" as he went out the door. *Ya Ya Ya,* he thought to himself as he checked his car before walking to the bus stop to go home.

Sharry thanked Lenny with a kiss when he came in the door. "What a wonderful idea Len. I really appreciate the opportunity to work with this woman. Heaven knows she needs it." Lenny looked at his usual spot on the couch and passed it up. "I think I'll sit at the dining room table tonight and have wine with a little candlelight!" Sharry ooooed and ahhhhhed while she led him to the dining room. They enjoyed talking about the case and how she can help with the recovery of the woman's life. "I'm very sure I chose the right caregiver for this woman."

Sharry smiled for the compliment. Len continued, "You know exactly what to do for people in need, Sharry. I mean that too." He looked suddenly serious, "Sharr, I'm not just saying this to make you feel good. You truly are the most loving, caring person I know."

Sharry looked into her wine glass and whispered, "Thank you, Len. I love you so very much." With tear-filled eyes of love she stood and hugged her husband for a long time.

Kyra lay on her bed in the dark room thinking of her friend Kat. She understood she's not the same right now. But at the same time, she just wants her back. Back as the same Kat she's always known. Thinking out loud, she said, "She has to be okay and get back to normal." Then there was a clunk in the other room. Kyra jumped off the bed and quietly grabbed the wooden walking stick she kept by her bed. Crouched and ready, she waited by the door of her bedroom. No one came. It got quiet again. Ky slowly opened her bedroom door but saw no one. She carefully went through to the kitchen. She checked the bathroom in the hall and turned to go back to her bedroom when

"SHIT!" She jumped with a start.

Jack said apologetically, "I'm sorry. I didn't want to wake you."

Ky dropped the stick and held her hand over her palpitating heart. "Don't EVER do that again!" Her mouth agape she went over and plopped down onto the couch next to him. "I thought we were taking a break?"

Jack worriedly said, "Well, yes and no. I need to take you to see Kat. They moved her to a rehabilitation center."

Ky, still agitated, said, "It's about time!"

Jack replied, "Hell yes, that girl's been through a lot of shit."

Ky put her head in her hands. "Can you take me to her tomorrow?"

Jack answered, "Yep, first thing in the morning before I start work." Ky thanked him with a kiss. Jack carried her to her bedroom, laid her on the bed, and quietly left the room and slept on the couch.

Sara/Kat woke early as she was used to doing at the farm. She got up and looked around the room. Very confused, she found the washroom but everything was so different. This is not her home. She heard her door open and crouched in the corner of the shower. The nurse coaxed her out of the bathroom and sat with her for a bit until she could get some bearings on her new room. Sara finally spoke. "Where am I?" The nurse explained the care she needs to feel better. "But I feel fine, I need to get home and see my sister—*where is my sister?*" she asked in alarm. The nurse gave Katherine her calm meds and called the psychologist for an immediate session.

Cara, Darci, and the two men, were still at the precinct answering many questions and asking for their sister Sara. The ladies were angry that she was taken away, but the captain knew it would be quite some time before they would be allowed visitations with Katherine Forrester.

The interviews with FBI agents and professional psychologists seemed to go on forever. They brought in each surviving member one at a time. Each recurring interview gave them a little more of the puzzle. After lengthy talks they addressed the Baur son with all of the evidence they had been compiling against him. He stood firm in his plea that it was all his brother and mother that made him participate in abducting the homeless people. The agents knew better. As soon as they could start interrogating the latest victim, they would have all they needed for court to put this fool away for the rest of his life.

Officer Stoller gripped his phone tight, while standing beside a deep pit. "Ah, captain, yer gonna wanna see this." The officers at the farm waited for the captain and FBI agents to get there before disturbing the evidence they found. The agents drove in, bringing the captain. They all hurried to the calls of the officers on sight. Pictures were being snapped while the agents huddled around the pit.

Agent Kratz threw a command toward the officer with the camera, "Make sure you get a copy of all these pics ASAP to my computer." The officer nodded and kept snapping.

Hurrtz lazily grumbled, "My God." He hollered for Stoller to get the coroner here ASAP. Then he shouted, adding, "Better tell him to bring help. And I'm gonna need a lot of soil samples." He stood scratching under his cap. "And get me a lot of samples from those burning barrels over there too. Gonna be a long night, gentlemen, I hope you brought snacks!"

They all stood around the pit staring into a deep pile of bones. Kratz shook his head and stated, "Well, I guess that little missing gal lead us to the rest of the missing people."

Detective Billings raised his brow and replied, "If it weren't for her, we probably would never have found them." Hurrtz gave some orders and walked away shaking his head. The extra agents stayed with the officers on sight to get as much immediate info from the coroner as they could.

The next week dragged on for all involved. The case blew into a news media feeding frenzy. The detectives and officers were ordered to mummy up and let the FBI agents deal with the reporters.

Katherine Forrester started to make some progress. She seemed to accept the fact that she must be Katherine as everyone keeps calling her so. She held her head in her hands as she tried hard to remember the things that Kyra had been telling her. The therapist smiled calmly at Katherine, "There is no rush for you to remember all of this. If your sessions get overwhelming, we can take a break for a couple of days. Give your brain a rest!" Katherine nodded agreement and the woman with the long brunette hair, that seemed to bounce when she moved, headed for the door. "WAIT!" Katherine stood and stared at her therapist with her hand stretched out. "Your hair."

The woman turned to look at Katherine with question. Katherine sat back down in obedience while her therapist sat. "Yes?" Katherine put her hand in her own hair and pulled on it. "I used to have hair like yours."

The woman smiled. "Well, that's a start! Go on."

"I used to tug on it when it was in my face ... and it was brown and silky like yours!" She smiled with confidence as she started remembering little things. The woman stayed another hour until Sharry Hurrtz arrived for her daily "pampering" she liked to call it. Katherine watched as the two women conversed in the hallway. She may be progressing but the hurt of losing her master and needing her sister Cara had not gone away. She knew deep in her heart, they never would. When Miss Sharr, as she likes to be called, came in, Katherine gave a big hug and confided in this woman what she cannot seem to do with her therapist.

Sharr patted the chair next to hers and smiled warmly. "You can talk to me about anything."

With that, Katherine poured her heart out of who she is and doesn't want to be this other person that everyone else wants her to be. Sharry offered, "I don't think they want you to be different ... just to remember." Sharry took her hands into her own and stated, "I and everyone else loves you just the way you are!" Then they giggled and Sharr took her to her room and brushed her hair while Katherine told her exactly what happened at the farm. Sharry just kept softly brushing her hair as Cara used to. As she told her story, Sharr's insides wretched and tears welled up in her eyes to hear such horror from a sweet innocent young lady.

Sharry spent most of the day coddling the young woman then went to the nurses' station to have a meeting set up with her husband, and the psychologist.

They met in a private room at the rehabilitation center where Sharry Hurrtz stated everything Katherine Forrester had told her.

Lenny took a recording of Katherine's story to the precinct for Kratz and Billings to hear.

At the local coroner's lab where FBI techs were assisting with the sorting and identifying of all the bones brought from the farm. Agent Kratz checked in on the progress, "Do we know how many different victims we have?" Dr. Ernest Geralds, a retired surgeon that became the local coroner for a slower pace, rolled his eyes. "Well, so far all I can say is, going back to surgery would be easier!" The room of chuckles gave a slight relief to the stressed task. Kratz bade to hold that thought for another day and left.

Tad Billings felt complete shame to the whole of mankind when he listened to Sharry Hurrtz's accounting of the tortures put on Katherine Forrester. It took all the restraint he had to not lash out at the nearest wall. Lenny Hurrtz stood and invited all to meet at the pub for some small talk and a few drinks to digest what they just heard. Tad replied with, "I'm definitely in."

The captain looked around the room and added, "Trust me men and women ... we need to work through this ourselves before we attempt to further this investigation." Everyone was looking everywhere but at him. "Folks! It's an order!" with that they all rose and headed over to the bar. Everyone ordered food on the departments bill and Lenny ordered the first round of drinks on him. "Now this is relaxing."

Sharry was part of that stampede over as she sat next to her husband. Len looked at her with sadness in his eyes. Sharry responded quietly, almost a whisper, "I know, I had no idea. That poor girl."

The whole day crew kicked back with their drinks and chuckled over anything but the case at hand.

Jack Burns walked outside to call Kyra. He made plans to sit down with her the following evening to discuss Katherine's progress. He thought to himself as he ended the call, *Tomorrow night I will tell her what happened to her best friend at that farm.* His place is where he went for the night.

Tad went back to the Center and once again slept on the cot outside Katherine Forrester's door. He knows now, all he wants in life is to keep her safe. *And hell or high water, no one is ever going to hurt this woman again.*

The court hearing for the other residents of the old farm was held and all four of the caretakers of the place were freed of any charges as they were not of the knowledge of the activities of the Baur family. All four were perceived as victims and released to the local shelter.

Cara O'Franks approached the lawyers on Sara's behalf, to question when they would be legally allowed to see her. Their lawyer looked confused. Sam stepped forward and corrected Cara with, "Excuse me, sir, what this dear lady means is, The Lady Katherine."

The man replied with understanding, "Oh yes. She has not been legally released. She needs to be certified, fit to approach the court." They were all looking at the lawyer with uncertainty. He then pulled over another lawyer to explain better. The lady lawyer took them all into a separate, quieter room. "This is much better!" They all four waited as she carefully and simply explained their friend's situation. Cara's tears were slowly trailing down her cheeks at the thought of not being able to see her, who she referred to as sister. The lawyer gave them hope with the plan of personally setting up a day with Katherine's therapist, a visitation schedule. Sam shook her hand and thanked her graciously as they all were transported to the shelter.

Billy Jud Baur finally broke down and told the truth of what him, his brother, and mother were doing to keep the business going. Any would be residents that refused to stay and become part of the family were taken to the barn and slaughtered with the cows and pigs. They supplied many surrounding county groceries with their meat. His brother Jo Bud Baur was the butcher. Billy, Pudge as family called him, was responsible to choose all livestock, including new residents. The Forrester woman was merely a supreme class of livestock that was supposed to go straight to the barn.

Their plan was botched when she escaped the shed and was taken into the house. In Billy Baur's words, "Jo went and got all smitten with the Miss Goody Two-Shoes bitch. Wouldn't even let me have a turn." The Baur prisoner was taken away in shackles and heavy metal cell doors slammed behind him. With the evidence gathered, which consisted of Alicine's prior warrants never served, her personal journal (her bible), two bunkers full of unlicensed weapons, a burned-up old green Buick behind the farm, the guillotine, and all of the human bones, Billy received his sentence of life in prison with no parole. The death penalty was not handed out as his brother was the one that killed all twenty-two victims at last count. The sentencing was lacking, according to the officers that helped process all of the evidence.

Kyra took the news of some of the horrible things that happened to her friend very hard. Sitting down with her and not bringing it up would be difficult. The therapist advised not to talk about it until Katherine was ready. Having a wedged secret between them was literally stretching them apart. Ky found herself distancing from her friend and spending most of her time with Jack. They had finally reunited completely, and were discussing making it right under God's eyes. They planned to marry the coming summer.

Spring was peeking out from the long winter of tragedies. The birds were singing in the mornings as Katherine lay in her bed waiting for Miss Sharry to come for her like her sister did at the farm. Although her door was not locked here, she still waited for Sharry's singing that made her realize how much she enjoyed Miss Mam's cheeriness in the mornings. She lay remembering Sam and Harry hammering on the broken porch and the hum of the barn as she swung her legs to the floor. Up and to the opened window. Still brisk in the mornings, she slept in the cold air just to awaken to the chirping birds.

She did miss her master and all of the attention he bestowed on her. Although not the fear of disappointing such a beast. With that thought so close, she slammed the window shut as if the devil were coming. Kat had gotten used to her previous name and was released into the care of Sharry Hurrtz. As a house guest, Sharry vowed this young gal to be the daughter they never had. Kat ordered her sisters and brothers would always be exactly that in her eyes. Sitting on the deck with Cara, who was there for a visit, Kat handed her the keys to her apartment.

Cara, confused, asked, "Do you need me to get more of your stuff?"

Kat shook her head and replied, "No, I want you and Darci to stay there until we can find a place for all of us to be together again." Cara teared up and hugged her sister.

"Are you sure?"

Kat answered, "Positive!" Cara was so excited to be able to get out of the shelter. Although very appreciated, it would give her and Darci a place to call their own for awhile.

"I better get back and tell Miss Darci!" She ran out in such a hurry she passed by Sharry without saying bye. Kat giggled when Sharry came on the deck with her hand over her mouth.

"What happened?" Katherine smiled and told her the plan. "Oh, that's wonderful!" Sharry paused, and then questioned, "Are you leaving me?"

Kat assured her, "Not now, but I am going to look for a place for all of us. I so love it here with you and Lenny." She paused with a sigh. "But I do want to be with my family again."

Sharry understood. "Family is always the most important people in our lives. Just don't ever forget that Len and I are also your family now. And where does Kyra fit into this equation?"

Kat answered, almost to herself, "I'm really not sure yet?"

Sharry added, "Well, she's at least your very dearest friend." Kat agreed as they sipped at some tea.

Tad came home with Lenny from work as he did nearly every day. They would all prepare supper and sit with wine by the fireplace. Kat thoroughly enjoyed Tad's coddling as he paid most of his attention towards her and how she was feeling that day. She thought how *he must get tired of me talking about my family*. She would try to talk about his life and family, but he always changed the subject to her. Until that night. Tad brought her a vase of flowers and took her onto the deck. It was cold by that hour but sweaters and light jackets did the deed. Kat shivered when Tad sat next to her. She immediately looked to the floor and froze in posture. Tad sensed the immediate change in her demeanor so he scooted to the other end of the rattan couch. He gave her his jacket, mostly to let her think her chills were caused by the cold. Kat stiffened again as he carefully wrapped his coat around her shoulders and then returned to the opposite end of the rattan. "I think it's going to warm up next week."

Kat finally looked up and smiled. He wasn't sure if her smile was due to the small talk and the warmth he gave her or the simple fact that he didn't expect anything physical from her. That criminal of a beast had ruined her. But ruined temporarily. He had every good intention for this woman. He didn't care how long it took. He would help her heal and someday trust a man again. Hopefully that man would be him.

As they sat listening to nature, Tad apologized for avoiding his secrets. Kat looked his way curiously. "I had a brother that passed away years ago in a car accident. And my mother and father are also gone. I can't expect you to do all the talking!" She smiled with understanding. "I had a fiancé in California where I'm from, but we broke up and I moved here." Kat gave another smile and nod of understanding. To himself he thought maybe she would open up to him about her feelings eventually if he did so. They sat awhile with another glass of wine and then he saw Kat yawn.

"You should get in from the chilly air and get some sleep. I'll be back tomorrow." He smiled and gave her a wink, as he followed her into the house. He made his good nights and went home to his loneliness. He stood looking out onto the balcony of his apartment. Only one block of lights to see. In San Francisco you could see lights for miles. And also hear the business. With a sigh, he shut the blinds to the lonely world and fell asleep watching TV.

Lenny was up at the whistle of a train going through town. Every morning it whistled at 5:00 a.m. All the years they've lived here, he's never needed an alarm clock.

He started the coffee as Sharry came dragging her heavy, sleep-deprived face. "Is it morning already?" Len chuckled and paused the pot to pour her some coffee. "Thank you," she said at a whisper. They were used to Kat sleeping in until Sharry woke her, so they sat at the counter in the kitchen with their coffee and quietly discussed the details of the ongoing legalities of the farm.

Still talking quietly Sharry expressed, "Can you believe it's already been almost a year since everything happened?"

"No."

"Len, I don't think we can ever tell her what happened to all those people. Thank God she has no interest in TV!" Lenny blew into his hands and shook his head as if he were cold.

"I think you and her therapist should tell her together." He hesitated and raised his eyebrows. "Before she hears some fool at the grocery store bring it up!"

Sharry hushed him as his voice raised a bit. Then she turned to a noise and jumped when she saw Katherine standing still as a ghost directly behind them. "What people?" Sharry looked to Lenny for support. Lenny turned his hand upside down toward his wife as a motion to move the conversation forward.

"Oh Len, I don't think this is the time or place to discuss all of that." Lenny replied, "Make the appointment, then." And off he went to work and left Sharry to explain to the woman gaping at her in determination to know the big secret. "I will make an immediate appointment for us to sit down with Mrs. Gernsey today." Sharry then got her ward some coffee and quickly left to shower." Kat stared at her coffee like it would be the last cup she would ever enjoy. She wasn't quite sure if knowing secrets is better than not knowing.

Lenny walked into the precinct and went straight to Tad's office. He shut the door and gave Tad a worried look. "Sharry is taking Katherine to see the therapist today to tell her the big secret."

Tad stared back. "Which one?"

Lenny raised his brow. "There's more than one?"

Tad quickly remembered he had never opened up about his previous engagement. "I'm sorry, of course you mean the barn activities."

Lenny flipped his hand over a few times with raised brows. "Yes, the dreaded barn conversation."

Tad questioned, "I thought we were sparing her that story?"

Len answered, "Well she overheard Sharry and me discussing things this morning."

"Ah," Tad said. "She was going to hear about the details from people sooner or later anyway."

"Exactly the point I made to Sharr this morning."

Tad put away the papers he had on his desk and stood. "I want to be there when this happens." Lenny gave him the okay to take the ladies to the therapist as a guide support. He let Sharr know to wait for Detective Billings.

The psychologist, Dr. Gernsey, a slender woman in her forties, with small round glasses at the end of her nose, had one slot left in her schedule for the day. She was more than happy to accommodate any progress in Katherine Forrester's case. She pulled Katherine's file and was brushing up on their last conversation when there was a light rap on the door. Dr Gernsey pulled her hair tightly back into a ponytail, as to not distract her patient with a memory she has already found. Each new item she recalled was of utmost importance to her developing progress. Her assistant, a short, bald man opened the door for Sharry Hurrtz, Katherine Forrester, and following behind was Detective Tad Billings.

Dr. Gernsey welcomed all and they sat in her therapy room of deep cushioned chairs. The session was scheduled to help Katherine manage knowledge of her captors' criminal behaviors. For Katherine, this would be difficult to digest, as she had developed Stockholm Syndrome. She was very emotionally attached to the master of the house, Joseph Bud Baur, and Alicine Fair Baur, which she knew as Miss Mam. To this point in her therapy, the people involved were not spoke of as criminals. Her session started with the facts.

"Katherine, do you understand that some of the people you were living with were involved in criminal activities?" There was a long pause and a look from Sharry to Tad, before answering Dr Gernsey's question.

She cleared her throat and stated, "Yes."

Tad, surprised at her answer, asked, "You knew?"

Dr. Gernsey looked to Detective Billings with reprimand., "We need to stay focused on Katherine only. You need to let me ask the questions." Katherine raised her arm as if in school. "Yes, Katherine, go on,"

"To answer Tad's question, ma'am, I knew that at least two of them were in trouble with the law, because they abducted me."

"That is correct, as we had discussed that previously, do you know all of the charges against the Baur family, which includes Miss Mam?" Katherine thought about it for a few minutes then answered, "Just that she shot and killed one of the officers at the farm the day the police came looking for me."

The doctor nodded, "Anything else you remember that may have been against the law?" She shook her head from side to side. "What we're going to tell you will be frightening and may cause you some emotional disturbances. Do you think you are ready to hear the complete facts involving you and people close to you?" Katherine braced herself, sitting higher in her chair and looked to Sharry for support.

"Yes, ma'am." Sharry held Katherine's hands in a motherly way. Dr. Gernsey turned to Detective Billings, "I will let you inform my patient of facts and evidence of her case."

Tad, surprised, straightened in his chair and began. "Miss Mam's given name is Alicine Fair Baur who had outstanding warrants for previous kidnapping charges and theft in another state. She was in charge of the illegal activities at the farm, which included the barn." Katherine felt a tear at her emotions as she looked to this woman like a mother. Sharry requested a moment to speak. The doctor allowed it.

"Please remember that you have all of us as your family now as you go through this." The doctor agreed. Tad moved on in his professional manner.

"Son of Alicine, Billy Jud Baur has prior arrests and outstanding warrants for kidnapping, theft, assault, and rape." Detective Billings looked to the doctor for permission to proceed.

She then looked to Katherine. "Do you need a few minutes or to speak?" Katherine held strong as Billy's list of no goods was no surprise to her. He was one she never formed any liking to. Detective Billings continued even though he knew the next subject would be the hardest on her.

"Joseph Bud Baur has a long criminal background." Tad glanced at Katherine to make sure she was still okay. He could see the emotion in her eyes as they welled up with soon to be tears. She tensed more than he thought possible. Dr. Gernsey motioned for him to please continue. "Jo as you know him, started young with a closed file. But at legal age he was imprisoned for aggravated assault, theft, involuntary manslaughter, and stalking. Then, of course, after he was released, he became a butcher. He also had outstanding warrants for kidnapping, armed robbery, assault with a deadly weapon and person of interest in two murder cases."

Dr. Gernsey paused the session to give Katherine a moment to process all of the information and to speak her thoughts. She let out an emotional sigh and leaned to Sharry for support. It was killing Tad inside to have to tell her all of this. He had an attraction to this young woman from the first time he looked at her eyes in that photograph, that to this day he still carried with him. Katherine now had tears trailing down her cheeks as Sharry held her tight. Dr. Gernsey advised she can handle this. She reminded Katherine how strength is how we survive these types of situations. With that, Katherine sat up straight and wiped the tears away from her face. Dr. Gernsey smiled and gave the detective a motion to carry on.

"The farm was used as a personal dwelling for the Baur family illegally. They took in homeless people to help run the farm. They butchered livestock to live on and to sell. There were human bones from twenty-two different corpses found buried in a pit behind the barn and ashes from the burning barrel also were from human remains. "Katherine had taken in breath but was no longer letting out air. She felt like acid and bile were traveling upward toward her mouth. She jumped from her chair and ran to the garbage can by the door. She heaved until it felt as if her whole being were extracted. Sharry ran to her as Dr. Gernsey also came to her aid with tissues. Tad froze in his own world of tortures from the past.

The doctor called the session to a halt. "In regards to Katherine's state, I am ending this session and will schedule a follow-up for Katherine in a few days. This will give her some time to process the situation. If however, she needs me sooner, please call the office and I will be on call." Sharry thanked the doctor for her time and guided Katherine out of the room. Dr. Gernsey approached Detective Billings as he seemed out of touch. "Detective, are you okay?" Tad snapped out of his trance and also thanked her for the session. She voiced after him as he was leaving, "I am here if you ever need to talk about things" Tad nodded and caught up to the ladies. He drove them straight home and returned to the precinct.

Sharry helped Katherine to her room. She set out clean towels in the bathroom and let her have time to shower off the emotions. Katherine sat on the bed and stared into nowhere until it all came surging back. Her mind was telling her to shut it out. It was too sickening and frightening to think about. But as hard as she tried, she just couldn't shake the horror of what happened to all of those people. She made herself get up and shower. Maybe Sharry is right, thinking she could rinse it all down the drain. So she did.

Sharry came to check on her and sat with her on her balcony as they tried to talk about the weather or the church banquet coming up. Then Sharry jumped up and shouted, "Let's eat ice cream!" She jolted a small giggle from her ward for the effort. They raced each other to the kitchen and overindulged.

Captain Hurrtz hollered for Billings to step into his office and close the door. Billings sat opposite his captain and informed him how the session went with the doctor.

Lenny pushed back in his chair and used his hand to wipe his face as if he had germs all over it as he updated Tad with the list of grocery stores that had to pull beef and pork from their cases due to the fact that they had purchased possible tainted meat from the Hockstead Farm. Tad looked confused at the name. Lenny explained, the new enlightened evidence from the FBI's further investigation of where the meat was distributed, that was supplied from said, criminal farm. Tad voiced, "I'm not quite sure I want to know."

Lenny half chuckled with sarcasm, "God, I love this job!"

Tad's only reply was "I need a few shots of whiskey"

Lenny jumped up and said, "Me *too*!" with much emphasis on too. "Let me check with the ladies first, then we'll call it a day.

Sharry and Katherine finished their much-needed binge on ice cream and went to the deck. Katherine turned to her confidant with hurt and sadness in her eyes, "I don't understand why God didn't save me from the things that happened."

Sharry looked up to the heavens and asked God out loud, "Why did you allow Katherine to go through all of those horrible things?" She looked at Katherine and smiled knowingly. "Simply because he knew you could handle what you had to go through to save more people from dying." She paused. "If you had never been there, they would have never found out what happened to those people and more would have died."

Katherine thought about it for a moment and replied, "I understand that, but they could've killed me!"

Sharry reached out and smoothed Katherine's hair as a mother would. "God is always in control and that is why you were spared." They hugged tight as Sharry's phone rang.

She answered quickly and Lenny said, "Wow, you must have been sitting on that phone!"

Sharry gave a giggle and replied, "Sweetie, I always know when my wonderful husband is calling!"

He chuckled at the other end. "You ladies up for the pub?"

Sharry looked to Katherine and replied, "You know what, Captain? I think some good food and a light drink or two is exactly what we need right now!"

Lenny motioned to Tad, *it's a go*, and they headed out to pick up their ladies.

The pub was always a bit crowded as it had the best burgers in town. The gentlemen seated their quarries at a table while they went to the bar to order food and drinks. Lenny asked Tad, "You think she looks okay?"

Tad looked into the mirror behind the bar as he always did. "Yeah, I think she's taking it all in slowly and doing as good as anyone would under the circumstances."

"Yeah, I guess."

Tad, still watching the ladies in the mirror, said, "I'll see if she needs to talk about any of it later after we get done here."

"Sounds great."

The bartender turned to the gentlemen. "Burgers and beers?"

Len looked at Tad as they replied in unison, "FISH! And whiskey!" The men raised their eyebrows to each other and chuckled. Small talk was the agenda, with a little laughter. Len told them all the story of when he was a kid and lassoed the family's pet goat. Katherine almost cried from laughter. She thought to herself, knowing everything now has released her from the hold the beast still had on her heart.

After the men were done chugging whiskeys, Sharry drove them all back to the house. They built a fire to relax and cuddle. It wasn't long before Sharry and Len bid their good nights and left Tad and Katherine alone by the fire. Tad said softly, "Please know that I'm here if you need to talk about anything." Katherine thanked him quietly, but assured him that she really doesn't want to ever speak of it again. He sat in his spot in front of the fire quietly until she said good night and went to her room. He had a gut feeling he should sleep on Len's couch that night, so he did.

At 2:00 a.m. Tad woke to commotion. Sharry heard a scream and ran to Katherine's room. Lenny jumped out of bed in nothing but his boxers. Tad hopped off the couch and went for his service gun. Katherine's screeching was the most dramatic and heart-wrenching thing he had ever heard. He also ran to her door to find Sharry holding the young woman like a child. She rocked her back and forth and cooed her out of her nightmare. Tears rolled down Katherine's face so steady she couldn't wipe them fast enough. He reached for the box of tissues by her bed and handed them out steadily.

Sharr looked at Len with worried eyes. Lenny just shook his head in pure sympathy. Then he looked at Tad holding his pistol by his side. "Good God, man, you planning on shooting someone?" Tad forgot he even grabbed it and looked down to his side as if the thing appeared there on its own. The men went to the kitchen after things were calmed down. Len grabbed a beer and handed one to Tad as they headed for the living room. Neither remarked on the event. They just rekindled the fire and drank their beers in silence.

The night never returned, as the sun came up, and the men were still sitting in the living room. Sharry started coffee and pancakes for all when Katherine came out of her room. Sharry said good morning with as much cheer as she could scrape up after a long night. Katherine tried a smile as she said her good mornings to Sharry as she busied in the kitchen and to the men that now came for coffee. They nodded and looked at Katherine like she was a china doll that was about to fall to its demise on a hard floor. Katherine found the whole of the situation comical all of a sudden. She let out a half cry and half laughter as they all looked on.

Officer Jack Burns made a formal announcement of marriage plans to the precinct. All were invited for the ceremony and party at the captain's house afterward. With summer coming up fast, they put together the announcements quickly, and found it was easier to just invite all verbally. Kyra made a visit to see Kat. Even though they had not been close since the abduction rescue, Ky still wanted her best friend of all time to be her bride's maid. She sat on the deck with Kat and sipped iced tea. Ky approached the wedding talk as if they had never had any interruption with their friendship. Kat was genuinely excited for her friend, but not to be a bride's maid. Ky assured her she would not need to do anything but be there to walk down the aisle for her. Kat hesitantly agreed. Kyra gave her hugs before leaving. Sharry threw Ky a wink as she passed, as assurance she would get her there for the ceremony. Kyra whispered a well-appreciated thank-you as she went out the door.

As summer came on, there was much excitement with a wedding in the planning. Sharry was very experienced in the party category. She left the ceremony to the younger crowd but the party at her house would be all her doing. She absolutely loved planning parties. She ordered the cake from an old friend that owned the local bakery in town and of course they must have flowers delivered from Nancy's Flower Pot on Main Street. The Breadstick Bouquet would have the fine honor of catering. It was all so very exciting to have this wonderful celebration to look forward to. The aftermath of the biggest crime scandal in the area was dreadful. But Sharry never doubted for a minute, that they would all come out on top of the world. Because she knew in her heart that when you have God on your side, everything here on this earth, no matter how horrible it seems, is so menial in the face of a joyous, perfect eternity with God.

Katherine's hair had grown out from the winter and Sharry had dyed it back to the original color. Though vanity is looked down upon, she was just thankful to have her own hair once again. She smiled to herself as she recalled Tad making a sweet comment about how pretty her hair is. Her heart just could not take any more hurt so she vowed to never get too close to any man again. It had become difficult to not lean on Tad as he always looked out for her. He occasionally seemed a little sweet on her. But she assumed he only felt sorry for her. As she stood in front of the mirror in her beautiful bridesmaid dress, she smiled a warm thoughtful feeling towards her lifetime friend that was about to take a man to her heart forever. The thought did seem wonderful, but she was still sad inside, knowing no man would ever want HER (Katherine Forrester) for she was surely damaged goods.

The ceremony was starting. Katherine went to join the gentleman from the precinct that was walking for Jack. It was not a large procession, just the two of them. As the music began, Katherine felt the jitters in her tummy. She looked out to the family and friends and suddenly stopped and felt as though she would faint. Sharry saw her quarry go pale as a ghost, so she pushed her way to the aisle and took Katherine by the other arm, opposite the best man and helped guide her down the aisle.

She stood as a human post for Kat as the bride and her father made their way to the altar. Kyra glanced a worrisome look toward Sharry and Kat. Sharry gave her one of her reassuring winks and they all smiled, for the rest of the ceremony was perfect.

Later at the party, Sharry pulled Katherine aside to whisper her thoughts on a certain, very finely dressed, gentleman that looked like he lost his new puppy. Katherine smiled knowingly and went to stand next to Tad in the same manner that he has always stood by her side. Tad looked down at her and offered a dance. Katherine looked nervous. She hadn't been close enough to anyone to really touch in such a way. Tad knew this, so he put his hand out with distance and bowed as a proper gentleman would. She smiled shyly and took his hand. They moved across the yard as if it were a formal dance hall. He twirled her and took her down for a quick dip. As he did so, their eyes met in a way that made her tingle all over. Embarrassed, and now overheated, she clung to him closely and hid her face in his chest. He didn't mind at all. He finally felt someone he loved against him and that was enough.

The party ended very late. Sharry announced to her helpers

that tomorrow or even the next day would be cleanup. She looked straight at Tad and Katherine when she bid, everyone to just hang out and enjoy the night. She smiled and went inside to cuddle with her husband. Tad looked deep into Katherine's enchanted eyes and whispered, "I love you." Katherine's heart began to race and she felt her legs giving out underneath her core. Tad felt her weaken and pulled her close for support. She wasn't sure how she felt at the moment. Trying to regain her posture, but failing, he picked her up and carried her into the house. Setting her down on the couch, he noticed Lenny and Sharry had vacated the living room. He knew what Sharry was up to, and was thankful for the little things she does to give them privacy. He wanted the same thing, a forever love with this woman who has scars he's not sure he can heal. But he didn't care about that. He just wanted to be with her and take care of her as any good man would.

Kyra and Jack had left the party a while ago, with their own private celebration at hand. They headed out to an island, with a cabana room on the ocean for their honeymoon.

Katherine couldn't help but think of the fond memories she had from the parties at the farm. She and Tad had danced like her and her family. She tried to block out the long nights she suffered at the hands of the master after their parties. Tad broke her thoughts when he cooed in her ear. She giggled and he gave a sigh of complete satisfaction. "How can you be so happy with so little?" He looked at her in confusion. "I mean, I've never imagined a man to be happy with just friendship."

Tad groaned in a deep voice, "My sweet lady, how can you profess my undying love as so little?" She giggled some more and brushed him off as teasing her. Tad gave her the most sensuous smile, she completely melted into him as their lips touched so gently. She thought she may faint. He lightly moved his lips over hers as if memorizing the feel of them for all eternity.

He whispered how perfect and beautiful she was and moved his lips to her ear. Katherine tried to catch her breath as she groaned softly. Tad knew if he didn't let up soon, there would be no turning back. He started to pull away but desperate for more, she pulled him back to her. She let out an irresistible moan of need. He warned her softly that he may not be able to hold back if she changes her mind. She didn't care anymore. She just knew she no longer wanted to go to bed alone. And she knew she wanted this man here in front of her, now. Tad stood, pulling Katherine with him gently. He picked her up in his arms and carried her to her room, where he carefully laid her on her bed. He bent over and gently kissed her on the cheek. He turned out the light and curled up beside her, fully dressed and held her close while they slept.

Late the next morning the house seemed quiet as Tad woke with Katherine's head still against his chest. He kissed her on top of the head as she stirred and asked, "Did you sleep well?"

Katherine sighed a relief and answered, "The best in a very long time."

Tad whispered, "I as well." Katherine thanked him for just being there. Tad smiled knowingly, that she was not ready for anything more. He proceeded to the kitchen and started a fresh pot of coffee, as Sharry and Len had already been up and gone.

Katherine held her head under the warm shower as she tried to wash away the memories of her previous life. If only she could make them disappear, maybe she would feel a deeper connection with Tad.

As she brushed her hair and dressed, the reflection in the mirror caught her eye. Out loud she professed, "This is me. Katherine Forrester. I am no longer Sara." With that statement, she turned in time to bump into Tad who was standing by the door smiling. "OH!" with her hand to her mouth. Tad wrapped his arms around her and just held her for a long time, kissing the top of her head. Katherine knew this would be a turning point in their friendship. "I think we should see Dr. Gernsey about…." She hesitated.

Tad finished the sentence, "Us and the fact that we almost did something last night that could set your therapy backwards." She looked up and nodded agreement.

Tad was filling their coffee cups and putting bacon and biscuits on two plates when Katherine sat at the table. She watched him like a little school girl with a crush on a boy. Tad caught her smiling and teased, "I so hope you like what you see, my lady!" Katherine looked away with a blush and tried to look busy arranging her eating utensils. He grinned to himself as he sat across the table from her. Small talk was shared and their ideas of what to do for a Sunday with no work to fret about. "We have to do clean up from the party"

Tad replied with a hand out in a stop motion, "No, I remember Sharry saying or the next day." Katherine agreed, so they made plans to go for a long walk and grab lunch at the deli café.

Sharry and Lenny had their own plans to give their newly coupled quarries some space for intimacy. She could not help going on and on to Len about Katherine's progress and her and Tad's relationship. Lenny looked at his wife with rolling eyes and commented, "Really? We have this whole day together and all you can talk about is other people's business?" Sharry sighed, "Len, you know how much I want those two together." He grabbed her arm and led her out of the church, thanking the pastor for the service. Sharry said, "We can't go home yet."

Lenny replied, "I wasn't planning on it." He then led her to their car and he drove them out of town.

"Where are we going?"

"To the farm."

Sharry gasped. "Oh Len, I don't want to see that place," she declared, shaking her head back and forth. Lenny kept driving and smiled at her. "Lenard Ray Hurrtz! You are pure evil!" "Sometimes." Sharr gave a huff and leaned into her seat with arms folded in defiance. Lenny turned down the dirt two track that led to the old farm. When in sight, he glanced at his wife and watched as her eyes got wide and she looked utterly amazed. There were trucks and people everywhere. She looked at her husband in disbelief. Lenny said with eyebrows raised, "Surprise!"

"What are they doing, Len?"

He answered with emotion, "I know how much you like to help people in need, so I got to thinking about this old farm sitting here empty again. I started making calls and got permission to purchase it."

Sharry exclaimed, "But, Len, I love our house and...." She paused. "It's our home!"

He shook his head in disagreement. "Not for us, silly!" She looked confused. He continued, "For Katherine's friends."

"Oh my God, Len! You are the most wonderful man in the world!" Tears welled up in her eyes as she sat in the car watching. Painters were scraping the outside to ready for painting. A furniture truck was delivering added necessities. Their friends were there working on refurbishing some of the current items in the house. Their insurance man was there doing estimates and taking inventory of all antiques and artwork. There were landscapers and the barn was being remodeled with much needed updates. The livestock was being inventoried and cared for. Sharry was now crying with such happiness to see everything he was doing for them. She turned back to Len and pulled him close to kiss him long and meaningful.

Lenny pushed her away and said with excitement, "Come on! I want to show you what your part is." She jumped out of the car and gave him a look of sheer anticipation. They practically ran to the farmhouse. Sharry giggled as she did a walk-through the old place.

"Oh, Len, Look at this old woodwork! And the velvet drapes! This had to be quite a popular place in its time."

Len pointed at things here and there in just as much excitement as his wife. "The original furnishings and décor will all stay. Some of it is being restored for value, but will be left in the house for use. They are using the value to borrow against for the repairs and upgrades needed."

Sharry was amazed at the details her husband has thought about and looked at him as a man she didn't even know. He pretended to not notice as he tried to keep wowing her. He bent down to lay a kiss on her cheek as he stopped in the tour to tell her what her participation will consist of.

"You, my dearest wife, will be picking out all the new linens, housewares, decorative pillows, any replaced curtains, etc., etc." Sharry teared up again. Len, with sarcasm, said, "Well, don't cry about it. I can get someone else to do it!"

"DON'T YOU DARE!" Sharr yelled.

Lenny snorted and chuckled as they proceeded to finish the tour. Then he guided her back to the car. "Now I know what a gossip monger you can be, so here it is. DON'T tell anyone. This is a surprise for Katherine and her friends." He gave her a serious look of possible penalty. She zipped her lips with a smile of agreement. Len headed back down the two-track and let her know their plans to go on vacations would come to a halt for a while.

Sharry noted and commented, "It's is well worth it."

Lenny gave her a very satisfied smile. "You know the best part of this will be the community has signed papers of agreement to have monies added to their taxes to pay for the upkeep and management of the farm from here on out.

Sharry further amazed, said, "That is so wonderful, Len. These people wouldn't be able to afford all of this." He nodded agreement.

"It's going to be classified a historical property and the historical society will be involved. And for the community it will be used for a homeless shelter with Katherine's friends living in and managing the place.

"What can I ever do to reward you for such a selfless wonder, Len?"

He grinned and replied, "I'll let you know later when we go home!" She playfully swatted him on his arm and snorted.

Summer in Lexville was beautiful. The Selkirk mountains could be seen in the far distance and the white pines were gorgeous against the backdrop of wooded and mountainous terrain. Tad drove Katherine to the lookout trail west of town. They packed a picnic lunch and decided they would eat lunch in town a different day. It was such a warm sunny day and perfect for a trail walk. Tad took Katherine's elbow to guide her along the trail. They wore bells on their shoes and whistles around their necks. Grizzlies are unpredictable near the mountains. Tad made sure he packed OFF! for the mosquitoes and bear spray in the picnic basket. Katherine leaned her head on his shoulder as they strolled along. She thought how wonderful it was to be with someone that is so caring, loving, and gentle.

A sigh of contentment escaped her as he pulled her tighter to him as assurance of security. They came along the little rest off the foot path, and he laid out their blanket on the ground for their lunch. He took her hand and helped her to the blanket. The birds were singing along and they could hear the summer breeze as it tickled the leaves on the trees. The mountain air was so fresh and clean, it made breathing almost purifying. They took out their lunch and took little bites in between small talk of nature. Katherine softly thanked him for this day. Tad smiled a welcome as he took her hand in his and quietly slipped a ring from his pocket onto her finger. Katherine looked at it with such surprise that she froze.

She just stared at the ring as if it were a symbol of dread. Tad said in almost a whisper, "Will you marry me Katherine May Forrester?" She teared up in eyes of emotion. Worried, Tad took her chin and turned her face to his. "This is a promise from me to you, to take care of you always and to love you like you deserve." He hesitated. "And Katherine, I love you more than you could know."

Katherine looked deep into his eyes as if trying to see if what he said was truth. "I know I would love to spend my life right here beside you, but I think we should talk to Dr. Gernsey about it." Tad agreed and kissed her long and gently. Katherine sighed with contentment as she pulled away. Then with a smile she answered, "I know I want this. I just need time." Tad dug into his lunch with a profound appetite. Katherine watched and whispered, "I want you, Tad Billings."

Tad looked at her with a serious stare. "I want you too. More than you could imagine. But,"—he took her finger, holding the ring—"not until we wed." Katherine nodded agreement, and Tad added, "I'm strict on that. I will, however, not leave your side except for work." She kissed him again and they finished their lunch and headed back down the trail to the car. Katherine could feel the smile on her face that did not want to go away. Tad held her hand in his as he drove them back home. Lenny and Sharry still hadn't come home. Tad went to his apartment to grab some more clothes and his personal items. He went back to the house and put his things in Katherine's room. Katherine looked at him quizzically. Tad explained with seriousness, "I told you I am not leaving your side except to work."

She replied with deep emotion, "Thank you." They hugged and made plans to go get dinner out and then surprise Sharry and Lenny with the exciting news.

Lenny took Sharry for pizza after their outing to the farm. With sore feet and feeling famished, they sat in the booth with a plop. "Oh my, Len, I haven't been on an all-day outing in quite a while."

"Me either!" Their pizza was put on the table as a familiar voice approached. Len teased, "Well, look who the cat dragged in! Are you lost, Vest?"

Agent Carson Kratz chuckled. "I'm never living that one down, am I?"

Lenny answered, "Heck no!" Sharry tapped the seat next to her as an invitation to join them. So he did. They enjoyed pizza and a beer when they heard another familiar voice.

"Hey, what do we have here?" Lenny jumped up and moved them all to a large table as Tad and Katherine joined the group. They announced their plans to the bunch and Katherine showed Sharry her engagement ring. Sharry cried happy tears as this news, she had been praying for. They left the pizza parlor and all went to the house. They enjoyed wine by the fire as it is always chilly in the evenings. They all chuckled and just enjoyed being together.

Morning came quick for Tad. He slept well being with Katherine snuggled in her bed. He wanted badly to take her in his arms and make passionate love to her, but that must wait. They hadn't set a particular date yet. He decided he would let the busybodied women figure that out. He let Katherine sleep in while he readied himself for work. Sharry had the coffee made and sweet rolls out for him. They sipped at their coffee and discussed wedding plans as Katherine and Lenny joined them.

Katherine felt overwhelmed all of a sudden and spoke out as if no one could hear her. "NO!" she half shouted. "I don't want any of that." Tad felt his world falling as though he'd been shoved off a cliff. He just stared at her, trying to understand what she means. She continued, "I just want to be married now. I don't want a wedding with all that fancy stuff and tons of people. Why can't we just do it now?" They all three stared at her now in understanding.

Sharry spoke with certainty. "Yes, yes of course you can. We would love to do it quick. Just tell me what you want, dear, and I will help you." Katherine calmed and thanked Sharry for understanding. They hugged and Katherine looked to Tad, "Are you okay with this?"

He put his arms out for her, and as they hugged, he said, "Most certainly. I just want to be with you. I love you." Katherine agreed and they made the arrangements for the marriage license and then with the pastor to come to the house. Tad never expected to be getting married so quickly. Lenny drove them both to work. Tad looked at his captain and friend and asked, "Is there anything I need to do before this takes place?"

Lenny just grinned and answered, "Pray?" They both chuckled.

The County Clerk's Office arranged the marriage license for one of their own, with great pleasure. With daily therapy for a week straight, the following weekend came quick. Tad picked up the papers and met up with Lenny, Sharry, and Katherine. Sharry had set up the backyard at their house once more, however with just her family, new and old members, Sharry was slightly disappointed when Katherine stepped in on her plans of a yard full of flowers and a caterer. She did however, allow her to flower line a walk to the pastor's mobile altar. It was still beautiful and every one present enjoyed party snacks and cake inside. The small, brief ceremony was romantic as Tad promised to take care of Katherine 'til the day she meets with the Lord. Katherine vowed to love Tad forever. They exchanged rings and kissed. In Katherine's mind it was perfect. Tad was completely satisfied to have the woman he loved, beside him forever.

With help, the newlywed couple moved their belongings to Tad's apartment, which they, for now, would call home. Tad helped his bride unpack, and then ate take out delivered from

The Breadstick Bouquet with candlelight. Tad leaned back in his chair and reveled in the thought, *I never dreamed I'd be sitting here in my apartment with the woman with the seductive eyes and also my wife.* He let out a satisfying sigh and stood. Then pulled her chair out and gently guided her to the window looking out on the small, quaint city. He pulled her close and took her lips to his. They kissed long and lovingly as Tad shared his view with the one he loved.

The progress at the community farm was moving along. The livestock was being doubled to ensure the residents would have plenty of stock to live on. The community met at the town hall to lay out the management plans. They knew very little of the four people that lived and worked at the farm previously. Keeping the element of surprise, as Captain Lenard Hurrtz requested, they would need to have the said residents do the same jobs as previously. It was voted and confirmed that Cara O'Franks would run the farmhouse. Which was more than she tended before, but with testimony from the current shelter it was decided, Cara would manage things just fine. Darci Redimere would have total control of the kitchen and menu plans. Sam LaFray would be the maintenance supervisor, and Harry Graden would be in charge of the grounds and barn, which included the livestock. They would all receive volunteer help from the community center until enough residents were added for helping. The meeting adjourned and everyone clapped and cheered, for it was one of the best community services they had ever put in place.

Captain Hurrtz's personal line rung at his desk. He stared a moment before answering it. That line is only for his officers and detectives to call privately with emergencies. He grabbed it quickly, "Captain here" The voice on the other end was raspy with emotion, but definitely Officer Jack Burns.

Hurrtz asked, "What's up, Jack, are you back early from the trip?" Jack hesitated a moment, then with grave difficulty, he answered, "No, sir, Kyra is missing."

The captain quickly stood from his desk, and with a loud voice he exclaimed, "WHAT?" There was silence for a moment as Jack tried to get a grip on his emotions. Before he could say anything else, the captain pulled his phone from his ear and hollered to Stoller and Billings. Stoller waltzed in lazily, and Billings practically pushed Stoller out of his way to get to the captain.

Billings voiced, "What's going on?"

Hurrtz quickly put the phone on speaker. "Okay, Burns, Repeat that."

Jack cleared his throat nervously, "Kyra is missing on the island." Hurrtz glanced at Billings with eyes wide and pointed to the phone. "I just wanted to make sure I was hearing you correctly." Burns said quietly, "You did, sir."

"What happened?"

"Sir, we were on the beach—" He hesitated with emotion. "—I ran into the room to get drinks and came back out and she was—" He sighed. "—gone." Jack tried to stay calm, but started to cry. His coworkers on the other end of the line all looked at each other with worrisome expressions. Tad Billings turned to go get Agent Carson Kratz. Lenny Hurrtz and Officer Stoller kept Jack on the phone until Kratz got on the line. Kratz took all the necessary information the FBI would need to get started on their case. They urged Jack to hang in there and Carson Kratz assured Jack they would find her.

They hung up the phone and Lenny wiped his face with his hand, squeezing the sweat out of his pores as he shook his head side to side and asked of no one in particular, "What the hell is going on?" Completely frustrated to finally find the missing gal in Lexville, but now another one is gone.

Tad Billings asked, "Who will you send?"

Captain Hurrtz let out a long sigh before hollering to Stoller and Wilks. He answered Tad, "I'll send those two for now. They can work alongside the locals and keep Jack under their wing. Kratz will send some of his agents down ASAP." Tad sat a moment while Lenny threw out orders to Stoller and Wilks. He put his clerk on getting the men plane tickets and paperwork. Tad offered, "I'll let Katherine know."

Lenny shook his head again. "That little lady has been through enough."

Tad agreed, "Yes she has, but she would be worse if it doesn't come from me." Lenny agreed and the men spread the news to be offering any support they can to Officer Burns."

Officer Jack Burns paced and paced some more, while the local police searched the couple's cabana room. He knew, as a policeman himself, they had to rule out foul play on his part first. They told him thoughtfully, "It's procedure. You know the drill." Jack finally sat down as someone handed him a beer. All day yesterday the police drilled him and he did not sleep the night. Officers Stoller and Wilks had just come in the room by the local captain's escort.

"Jesus Burns, you look like hell." Wilks gave his insensitive partner a crude look. Stoller brushed him off saying, "What? He can handle it! He's a big boy and he's strong. In fact, you couldn't take this guy down, He's steel man."

Jack replied with a forced chuckle, "Don't forget it!" Stoller grabbed the out reached hand from Jack and shook it hard as he pulled him to his chest.

"Don't you worry, son. We're not going home without her."

Jack swallowed his emotions and stiffened up. "Damn straight."

The three sat at the room's kitchenette counter. They went over any witness statements and Jack's recap of events. "She wasn't depressed, or unhappy. In fact, she told me just that morning she was the happiest she's ever been. She didn't say anything about going in the water or to the beach restroom. She was laying in the sun when I left her to get us some drinks."

Stoller asked with care, "Did they search the water?"

Jack answered with worry still crossing his brows, "Yes. They even noted no sharks nearby."

Stoller then approached the witness statements. "People saw a man. Large man talking to her. Are you absolutely sure—" He paused and continued gently. "—She would not have followed him somewhere?"

Jack responded quickly, "Absolutely not! She's smart. She would never go with a stranger willingly. Especially not away from home." Stoller agreed and continued, "There were several witnesses that stated they were distracted with a swimmer in distress. We'll have to assume that's when he grabbed her and quite obviously covered her mouth. Being large, it would be fairly easy to carry her off." Stoller paused in thought. "I mean, she probably weighs all of a hundred pounds?"

Jack thought for a minute, "Yeah, I think she said she weighed about one twenty-five when I carried her over the threshold." Stoller nodded and they all stood with plans to eat a bite and go talk to the witnesses again.

Finishing their Po'boys and beer, Jack stared into the bottomless ocean with dread. Stoller snapped his fingers in Jack's face. He came out on a stoop and stood to join the other two men in haste. They approached the waiter at the small island tiki bar with questions and a photo of Kyra. He hesitated in thought but then answered with a shake from side to side. The men thanked him and went on to the next hut. A shell and bone jewelry hut. Stoller in charge was the one who asked the questions and showed the picture. The elderly woman dressed in a colorful gown and much jewelry recognized the photo. Jack pushed forward between Stoller and Wilks.

"Where?" he almost shouted. The woman pointed to the beach. She put her arms up in the air as she imitated the girl in

the photo. "She do dis, and hit man." The men asked her to de-
scribe the man. The woman waved her hand around in leisure
and looked up as she assured them, "He no hurt her. Juss play.
Packy." The three looked to each other in confusion.

Stoller questioned the elder. "You know who he is?" The
woman nodded yes. She pointed to the hills behind the small
village.

Stoller and Jack asked in unison, "Where?"

The woman called out to a boy. "Com com, Hejee!" The
men watched as a young boy came out of the bushes.

"Yaya." They waited as the woman explained the situation.
The boy giggled and took Jack's hand and led him to a trail. The
men followed as Hejee escorted them up a trail into the tropical
jungle. They kept close to the boy as to not get lost. Strange
birds made loud noises and they dodged around vines that
looked like snakes. They looked at each other in uncertainty of
their surroundings.

Stoller gave Jack a questionable look, "You just had to come
to the jungle for a honeymoon?" Jack looked every bit regretful.
Wilks pointed up ahead to a small shack and near a small water-
hole. The boy excitedly ran toward the shack exclaiming, "DeDe,
DeDe," A very large, yet boyish-looking man came out of the
shack as the men approached. Stoller held out his hand to greet
the man. He said nothing but mussed up the boy's hair in play.
Hejee asked the man about the girl in his own sort of language.
He took the picture of Kyra from Stoller and showed him. Hejee
then turned to the men and introduced the large man as Packy.

Jack nodded and looked to the man. He put his hand out to
him saying, "Packy" then put his hand to his own chest and said,
"Jack." Packy smiled and repeated Jack. Hejee spread his arms
out in question of the girl. Packy pointed to his shack and said
to the men, "Mi" They started to walk toward the shack and
Packy stepped in their way. "MI!" Hejee turned to the men and
explained Packy. "He keeps her."

Stoller turned to Jack, "Try to explain to the boy about your wife." Jack showed Hejee the photo of Kyra again and explained her as his heart, meaning love. He tapped her picture and his heart gently at the same time. Hejee understood. He took the picture of the girl and tapped it to Jack's chest. "Maui He He!" Packy nodded with sadness as he led them into his shack. It was a small shack but very clean inside. Filled with all kinds of shells and coconuts. He had a bed of palm fronds in the corner and a makeshift table that held handmade dishes of petrified wood.

Jack tapped the photo again and spread his arms out in question of where. Packy took them out the back door to the water hole. Jack gasped as he saw Kyra laid out on a bed of palm fronds and sticks. She wasn't moving. The men all ran to her and Jack immediately checked for a pulse. "She's alive! Barely but we need to get her to a hospital NOW!" He picked her up and carried her back to the cabana as Stoller got on his phone. Wilks ran to the elderly woman's hut and asked her for a hospital or doctor.

She nodded and took him to another hut. Wilks sighed in frustration as a man in tribal garb came out. He motioned for him to follow as they ran back to the cabana where Jack was washing Kyra with cool wet cloths. The tribal doctor approached Kyra chanting tribal language. Then he took the water from Jack and put some into his mouth and put his mouth over Kyras. He parted her lips with his and let the water seep into her mouth slowly. He motioned Jack closer and gave the water jug back to him. He put his hand to his mouth and then to hers in a motion of instruction. Jack nodded and took over the approach. The tribal doctor then ran out and returned with a poultice of herbs and warm cloth. He spread it over Kyra's body and continued chanting. Stoller put his phone away and let the others know a med buggy was on its way from the nearest city. Kyra started to come around.

Confused and scared she looked up at Jack. Without a word

she grabbed him and squeezed so hard he could hardly breathe. "It's okay, we found you. You're gonna be fine." Ky started to cry. "I want to go home, Jack. Right now!"

He answered softly, "Yes, we will. As soon as I get you checked out at the hospital." He attempted to stand, but Kyra pulled him back down and refused to let go. "It's okay, Ky, I'm not going anywhere without you. Ever again!" She cried some more until the medics arrived. Jack sat next to Ky as the medics checked her over. They gave a good report with only dehydration being a problem. Jack agreed to wait a day before taking her on the plane for home. The medic said she needs a day of fluids and rest first. Stoller and Wilks stayed so they could all fly back on the same flight.

Stoller looked at the newlywed couple and stated, "I am not letting you two out of my sight until we step foot on US ground! So looks like the honeymoon is over!" They all laughed and ordered food and drinks from the tiki bar.

Cara and Darci had been comfortably living in Katherine's townhouse and working with the shelter they once called home. There were not as many people in need as there once was. All the same, their help was still needed. They had just returned home from the farmers' market with plenty of fruits and vegetables to make a healthy salad with fruit on the side.

Along with the fresh baked chicken they received from the shelter, Cara offered, "We should invite Katherine and Sharry over to eat with us!' Darci was tearing lettuce into a dish for the salad when she agreed. Cara called and Katherine accepted for the two of them and Tad drove the two of them over to Katherine's old apartment. He left as Sharry and Katherine walked up the sidewalk to the door. Katherine stopped suddenly with a look of fright on her face. Sharry asked, "What is it?" Katherine in panic turned and ran down the street. Sharry tried to catch up as she called Tad on her phone.

"Somethings wrong! Come back!" Tad didn't take time to question. He squealed his tires in a U-turn and dodged vehicles while racing back to where he left the two. He didn't see either, so he jumped out of the car and pounded on the door of the apartment. Cara opened the door quickly, as she could hear by the pounding, something was wrong. She took one look at Tad and knew it was something with Katherine.

"What happened?"

Tad said, "Are they inside?" Cara shook her head in confusion. Tad didn't explain he just ran back to the car and squealed his tires once more to find his wife and friend. Tad's nerves were wrenching his insides. *Nothing else can happen to her.* He knew how much he loved this woman even though it made no sense. He barely knew her and now they are married. He vowed to take care of this one. He swore he would never let his past repeat itself. As he drove he caught sight of Sharry frantically looking for Katherine. He stopped and yelled out his window to her, "Get in!"

Sharry obeyed and they continued on as Sharry explained what happened. "She just froze outside the door like she saw a ghost!"

Tad assured Sharry, "In her mind, she did."

"Oh, poor girl." Sharry just held her hand to her chest in worry. Tad spotted Katherine by the river's edge. He watched as he left the car and told Sharry to wait there. She was sitting there covering her face and rocking as she sobbed. He approached slowly and whispered as he touched her shoulder so as not to frighten her.

"It's me, Tad." Katherine turned to look at him with saddened wet eyes. She said nothing and looked back to the water. Tad just sat next to her quietly and waited. He knew she needed to process the night she was abducted. The therapist had warned of this happening. Her vivid memory of the event had been replaced by the attachment of her captor. Dr. Gernsey had said she would start remembering events as they were, now that she wasn't under the spell of her captor. He knew that alone would put her over the edge. Just knowing that she fell in a weird kind of love with a murderer and became part of a family of criminals was enough to put anyone into a world of disbelief.

Tad didn't care about all of that. He just wanted to be the one that was there for her and to hold her close no matter what happened. Katherine reached for his hand and Tad held hers. When she was ready, they stood and he guided her to the car. Inside, Sharry looked at Katherine with understanding and motherly love. Tad dropped Sharry at home and took his fragile bride home. Cara and Darci agreed to come by Sharry's the next day to sit outside and have tea, in hopes that Katherine would be up for some womanly support. Tad sat at the kitchen table with Katherine. He made her some hot chamomile tea and took a beer out of the fridge for him.

They sat sipping their drinks in silence. When she was finished with her tea, Katherine stood and went to their bedroom. Tad followed and watched as she routinely stripped off her clothes and waited dutifully for what followed. He thought to himself, *Good God, is that what it was like? It's no wonder she has no idea what a real love and intimate relationship is.* He was as much a man of need as any other, but he knew they were not ready for this in their marriage.

Using every bit of self-control as he could find in himself, he lay next to her on their bed and covered her with a blanket. Then he whispered gently, "I want very much to make love to you. But I want to wait until it is just us. No past. No Sara. I want only Katherine. Whoever Katherine may be, just not Sara. "Katherine looked confused. She put her hand over his loins and kissed him vigorously. Tad groaned with discomfort. He pulled her hand away and held it as he stared into the eyes of Sara. He leaned toward her and gently kissed her back, but with a love filled desire and not a need for sexual release. Katherine returned the kiss but pulled off the blanket and laid herself out as a trained slave. Tad sighed and covered her back up, stroking her beautiful hair and touching his lips softly to her head in a comforting way. She fell asleep.

The next day everyone met at Lenny and Sharry's house. Cara and Darci came as promised and Tad and Katherine were there. They all had iced tea and beer. It was a warm day with the mountain peaks far but in view. They chatted about things ahead and plans to take a weekend getaway together as a family. Lenny had just thrown steaks on the grill when a foursome arrived bearing more food and beverages for the party. Lenny hollered out announcing the newcomers. Sharry jumped up to welcome Jack and Kyra back to the real world. Lenny watched the steaks as Stoller told the exciting story of how a groom lost his bride on a tropical island.

Of course, he was the hero that solved the case of the missing lady from the beach. They all laughed when he explained the big childlike man that just wanted a real-life barbie doll to play with! Katherine glanced at Kyra in notice of her quiet tone. She went over to sit by her and offered her support, as they had both suffered similar circumstances. They spoke quietly as they chatted, understanding. Sharry noticed the two and elbowed Tad who was sitting next to her. He looked at the two getting along and smiled at Sharry in knowing. Lenny announced he had a little surprise for everyone tomorrow after church. With that, they all bid good nights and everyone departed with a promise to meet at church in the morning.

Jack put his exhausted wife to bed and crawled in beside her. She cuddled close and made him promise to keep her safe. He made love to her and kept his service pistol on the bedside table. Kyra slept soundly for the first time since returning home.

Tad and Katherine sat up awhile. Katherine unloaded Kyra's story onto Tad and seemed to feel better about their relationship. The therapist told her to concentrate on the relationship they can build now as opposed to the previous one. She assured her husband it was working. She continued talking as if Tad were her own personal therapist. He didn't mind one bit, as he was just grateful to be a part of her world.

"It's all so confusing Tad. I don't know who I am anymore."

Tad brushed her hair out of her face with his hand as he broached the subject. "It doesn't matter who you were, or who everyone thinks you are." He took her chin in his hand and turned her face to his. "All that matters in the whole world is you are mine and your life with me is all you need to think about." Then he leaned in and kissed her so romantically she groaned this time. Katherine tried to brush the overwhelming need of him away, but it was getting harder and harder to avoid.

"I know you want to wait to make love—" She hesitated with a sigh. "—but I really just need you right now." Tad looked deep into her soul as he stared into her eyes. Finally, what he had been waiting for was looking back at him. As if their two souls were the only beings on this earth. He never took his eyes off hers, as he took her hand and led her to their bed. Katherine thought she would faint as he kept her eyes on him and seductively kissed her lips with more passion than she could ever imagine one having. He very slowly unbuttoned her blouse and dropped it gently to the floor. Then he carefully unzipped her skirt and let them fall. She gave a whisper of excitement that sent him into a reeling passion. He quickly shed his clothes and pulled her to him while he removed her bra and panties.

He felt a surge of need as he laid her down onto the bed. Enjoying every inch of her with gentle kisses. He started at her neck and moved his way down, bringing sudden gasps of arousal from her as he got to her loins. Tad was so erect, but held back as he wanted to bring her to her highest peak before entering.

It was so very difficult, for he had waited so long for this. He gasped with torture as she began to rock to his motion. She pleaded for more and suddenly lost control with the most wonderful orgasm she'd ever experienced. Tad entered her with caution, but with his own need for release. He moved with her and climbed higher than he thought possible. He kissed her with such passion as he let go and filled her with so much love and passion she started to cry.

He whispered in her ear as he lay spent against her. "I hope those are happy tears?" She giggled a little and confirmed with a new arousal beginning. She moved against his leg until she satisfied her need once again. Tad cupped her breasts and throughout the night they repeated their passion as many times as needed before finally sleeping. Tad awoke while Katherine was still sleeping beside him. He looked at the clock and realized they were missing church. He lay back down and snuggled his bride close. She squirmed a bit as he put his lips softly on her breasts and reached down for that sweet spot. She started to breathe short needy breaths and came to a full climax as he entered her bringing him to a hard fulfilling climax.

He pulled her close and kissed her all over, repeating how much he loved her before pulling her out of the bed. "We missed church; they'll be calling to check on us." Katherine smiled and went to shower. Tad took the call and assured their friends they were fine and getting ready to join them soon. He then joined his beautiful wife in the shower. They made love again under the streaming water and then washed each other gently.

The others were all back from church and hanging out at Lenny's when Tad and Katherine arrived. It was a large crowd as Lenny had invited local contractors and business people. He also had Sam and Harry brought out for the announcement. Tad went to the patio bar and made two long island iced teas.

Lenny looked at the smile on his detective's face and the

drinks in hand and chuckled a little. "You look like you may be celebrating something!"

Tad replied, "You know, you just may turn out to be as good a detective as I am some day!"

Lenny laughed loud and let the man through with an announcement. "Folks, I have a surprise to show you." Sharry clapped her hands with excitement as she knew the surprise. Lenny threw his eyes her way with a "SHHH." So she hushed and let Lenny have the floor. Since it was his doing completely. He went inside the house and brought out a large board with pictures and pamphlets.

"In regards to my sweet lovely adopted daughter, Katherine May. I decided to do this here. It may have been a bit much to take you all to the place." He held up the board and continued, "This, my friends is the new community-owned and operated shelter for all in need." Lenny was holding up a diagram of a very large farmhouse. He then went on to explain the situation at hand. Some cheered and some looked confused. He then announced the paid positions that would be filled by the previous tenants. Sam turned to Cara and they hugged Darci in group form. Clapping all the while and cheering. Harry looked to Lenny with a positive nod of acceptance. All was well for all. Everyone talked in their own circles of the plans and time frame. Tad looked down at Katherine as he noted a stiffening in her demeanor. She was staring at the picture of the farmhouse in recognition.

He whispered to her ear only, "How about we take our own party elsewhere?" She nodded silently as she passed by Sharry with a quick hug and polite dismissal. Sharry hugged her tight and bid complete understanding. They left as the party continued. Tad drove them to the ice cream parlor before turning into their parking spot.

Katherine spoke out. "No! I need to face all of this. I need to see it now and with just you." Tad agreed that would be a good idea since her sisters and brothers would be living there once again.

"Promise you will keep in mind, the evil is gone. All of it. It's just a new house now." She nodded, accepting the new story to replace the old.

The two drove to the farm in silence. When coming down the drive way, Katherine stiffened. Tad stopped the car. "Are you sure you want to do this?" She replied with a nod. He continued until the farmhouse came in sight. He stopped again and waited. They sat in the car for a few minutes, taking it all in. The farm itself was different. The fences and barn were all new. There were caretakers there still working on the front walk and the gardens. Katherine noted the old shed was gone and replaced with two brand-new ones. The house was the same but repainted and held new shutters and a new front deck that was well furnished for enjoyment.

She looked to Tad as she took it all in. He asked, "Want to go closer?" She silently nodded. They parked and approached the house. Tad could feel her hand squeezing his as they went inside. Katherine looked around and noted the original wood carvings were all the same but restored. She turned to Tad and began talking about the first time she entered the house. He let her talk all she wanted, as it was considered therapy. As they toured the house, Katherine's full memory of the place returned. She went on about the waltz parties they had and the meals shared. She started to pull him along in excitement of it all. Tad let her.

She told of how Miss Mam was so kind and sang out loud as she worked. They went upstairs as Katherine saw everything as it was then and not how it looked in front of her. "This is Cara's room, she locks my door behind me, per the master's orders, of course. And this is Miss Darci's room. She loved to have her window open all of the time so she could hear the birds in the morning." She looked right at Tad, but he swore she was looking right through him. He knew she had gone back in time when she started referring to everything as present tense that was in fact past tense and no more. He also knew that she would be crashing back at any time while they were there.

He always told himself he was ready, but every time she had a memory event, he also crashes right with her on the inside. Katherine took Tad to the rest of the rooms, explaining who slept there. Then at the other side of the hall near the stairs she stopped. She threw her hand to her mouth and gasped. Tad tried to touch her and she screamed at him to get away. She put her hand on the closed door in front of her and dropped to her knees and wept. Tad was suddenly feeling overwhelmed with how to handle this. He stepped back and keyed Sharry's number into his phone. She picked up with a loud party going on in the background.

Tad tried to speak quietly so to not disturb Katherine. He went down the hall and stepped into a room as he explained where they were. Sharry took a deep breath of worry.

"Stay there, Len and I will bring Cara and Darci. Maybe they can bring her back around." He hung up and went back to where he left Katherine. She was gone. He tried not to panic, but his stomach was doing flips as he checked all the doors upstairs. Even the one they hadn't entered that he was sure must have been hers. She wasn't there. He ran down the stairs and asked a man that was going through to the back porch. He hadn't seen anyone. He checked the rest of the downstairs and did not find her. Feeling more of a panic he went out the front and asked the ladies working in the front flower gardens if they had seen her. They had not.

He ran back in the house and checked all of the closet doors he could find. The door off the kitchen, the cellar he had forgotten. He opened it. A flash of the night they rescued her came to mind. He went down the stairs and slowed as he saw her on the cold floor of the cellar curled in a ball with all of her clothing in a pile beside her.

With much urgency, he knelt on the floor beside her and caressed her hair as he whispered, "It's okay. I'm here. We can stay here as long as you need." He huddled his body around her to keep her covered and warm. She lay sobbing as if to herself.

Sharry's voice calling out made him move to see the stairs. As she, Cara and Darci topped the stairs, he waved a hand to summon them down. When Sharry saw the condition Katherine was in, she gasped and got on her cell phone to summon Dr. Gernsey for a house call. Cara knelt quietly beside her sister, caressing her hair softly, as Darci looked on. It was a good hour before the doctor arrived. Katherine was still in the same fetal position and Tad did not break away from her until the doctor motioned him to. They all left the cellar leaving the doctor and Katherine alone. She talked soothingly as she coaxed Katherine to come off the floor.

She questioned her if this was where he punished her. Katherine nodded slowly. Dr Gernsey helped her up and reminded her that this is all in the past now. As she helped her redress, she comforted her with assurance she would never suffer that punishment again. It is over. She had done nothing wrong. Those people tricked her into thinking she was to blame for all that happened. They were wrong. She did nothing to deserve that. Katherine trusted the doctor. She agreed with nods and let her lead her up the stairs. She handed her off to Sharry so she could talk to Tad alone. They stepped outside and she gave him a sedative to take home with them.

"Make sure she takes this when you get home. It was a sizable event she worked through. But no need to worry, she needed to face this and get past it. I believe she has." She hesitated. "But bring her tomorrow to see me. I need to see how this has furthered her therapy." Tad agreed and thanked her gratefully. He went to Sharry and the girls and thanked them as well. Sharry gave them both hugs and walked them to their car. The volunteers had all went home by the time Tad was ready to drive them home. Katherine stared at the house as he turned the car around. She seemed a million miles away.

When home, Tad sat Katherine down to tell her his experiences from the past. He hoped it would help her realize everyone has a past to work through. "I was engaged. Yes, I was once in love before you. But nothing like our love," he assured her. "We had been dating a long time, and I guess we assumed to marry eventually. We were never close like you and I. But she left." Katherine consoled him with a gentle touch on his arm. "That wasn't the bad part. She then died, and I've always felt I let her down and didn't take care of her."

Katherine shook her head in disagreement, "Not true! You are the most caring loving person I've ever met."

He thanked her with a kiss and added, "So now you understand why I am so protective of you?" Katherine pulled him to their bed and cuddled as she slept.

Two weeks had gone by and Katherine showed no signs of regression. She seemed happy to be living in the present with all of the bad memories behind her. She had been to the farm a few times now helping Cara and Darci and the men get settled. A few helpers had moved in as well. Cara was enjoying being in charge of making sure everyone was taken care of. Darci only allowed one other helper in her kitchen. She said to Cara, "This might be a large kitchen but it's mine and I need room to work!" that being said, Cara had to laugh, and she willingly left all kitchen matters to her sister. In Caras eyes, everyone that passed through or stayed was either a sister or a brother. She made sure Miss Mams book was never spoke of but replaced with the Holy Bible. Bad omen she would say. Everything was much better than before.

Tad and Katherine talked of buying a home close to Lenny and Sharry. They live in a nice neighborhood where backyard parties were common. Their love had grown very deep while working through Katherine's experiences. Her and Kyra have been working on their new relationship and going on double dates with her and Jack. Kyra had announced at the latest party that she is now pregnant with their first child. And she was also excited to say they know it will be a boy and his room is all set up and ready. Everyone cheered and drank a toast, excluding Ky.

CPSIA information can be obtained
at www.ICGtesting.com
Printed in the USA·
LVHW081330180922
728651LV00014B/639